More Thoughts
While Walking the Dog

Stories

by
Lynn Ruth Miller

excentrix press
Street Saint Publications
Pacifica, CA 94044

Published by:
excentrix press
441 Brighton Road
Pacifica, CA 94044
ISBN 1-931090-98-X

Cover Design
by Barbera / Arnaudie Design Group

Photography
by Rod Searcy

Dedicated to Elaine Larson
with love and appreciation
For loving these stories
and tending to the well being of their writer.

In Appreciation

A note of thanks to the people of Pacifica who read many of my stories first as columns in The Pacifica Tribune and wrote letters of encouragement, praise and love to the author.

A chord of recognition must sound for Eleanor Tomic and Kathleen Beasley who have always believed in my work and encouraged me with letters and words of lavish praise.

The most credit for the birth of these fantasies belong to Monsieur Donald Poodle, Amy, my liberated woman and Dorothy, my Jewish Princess along with my nephews Toby Poodle and Paul Chihuahua. All have been ever-loyal companions on these walks and the catalyst to the thoughts that spring to my mind as I monitor their habits and observe their unquenchable joie de vivre.

And a reminder to all of you that it is our differences that are our most valuable contributions to the human condition. Dare to defy your traditions. We will all benefit from your originality.

- Lynn Ruth Miller

Table of Contents

More Thoughts While Walking the Dog

Pacifica's Lynn Ruth Miller of is a tireless bundle of energy who is constantly exhibiting her paintings, doing book readings, or hosting special community events. Whether you see her at the Rotary Club's Dog Contest, or telling her stories before library audiences, Lynn Ruth's joie de vivre rubs off on all around her. She proves through example that it's never too late to pursue your creative dreams. Indeed she is an inspiration to everyone with her can-do attitude and boundless spirit.

Her first book, THOUGHTS WHILE WALKING THE DOG, published by excentric press in 2001 is a collection of many of her Pacifica Tribune columns. These heart-warming, slice-of-life stories about her childhood and adolescence growing up in a Jewish household in Toledo, Ohio chronicle the pitfalls of life in the 1940s and 1950s with pathos and humor.

This new collection, MORE THOUGHTS WHILE WALKING THE DOG, continues her trademark storytelling style, capturing the joys and heartaches of life, stories that are universal in their insight and appeal.

Dog lovers will enjoy her tales of growing up with an assortment of canine friends, holding neighborhood parades on holidays or family picnics in the park. There are equally charming stories that deal her life growing up in a first-generation American ethnic family with its cast of eccentric family members and friends.

Travel back in time with Lynn Ruth as she relays accounts of her Romanian grandmother's life as a young bride, and later when little Lynnie Root was the apple of her grandmother's eye. Experience Lynn Ruth's humorous sagas of coping with adolescence in the 1950s, her schoolgirl crushes, her struggles to deal with an overbearing mother, and her later successes and discoveries as an elementary school teacher.

Part autobiographical, part whimsical, Lynn Ruth Miller's original collection of story vignettes hearken back to early Americana when oral histories told at your grandmother's knee provided the basis for life's greatest lessons.

Elaine Larsen
Assistant Editor
The Pacifica Tribune

Acts of Kindness

Kindness is the golden chain
That binds society together
- Goethe

Every woman knows that "I love you" implies so many things that unless you are omniscient, the phrase is meaningless. In my idealistic youth, I believed that somewhere out there was a sincere human being who would adhere to the dictionary definition of those three words when he whispered them in my ear. Alas, I never found anyone whose professed devotion lasted longer than a summer rain shower or an evening in the sack. While I searched and hoped, dozens of strangers and hundreds of friends did beautiful favors for me every day, but fool that I was, I didn't think those acts of kindness meant love.

Now that I am older and understand reality, I know that it was those very strangers who offered me the real thing. They showed commitment not just to me but to all humankind and their goodness enriched us all.

I was given my most poignant gift of caring the year I decided to travel around the country in a fifth wheel trailer with my two dogs, Molly and Cindy and my cat, Eileen. I was in Winnfield, Louisiana on my way to Natchitoches for their annual Thanksgiving Festival when I had my first mechanical failure. I pulled into a service station to refill the fuel tanks, but I misjudged the distance between the pumps. If I continued forward I would crash into a waiting automobile. If I turned to the left I would hit the gas station. I threw the truck into reverse, the trailer bucked like an angry stallion and everything stalled except my nerves.

While all this was happening, a man I did not know was leaning against the side of the station watching me try to negotiate my massive vehicle into the narrow corridor. He knocked on the cab window of the truck and said, "Can I help you, Miss?"

Help was the understatement of the hour. "Rescue" would have been far more appropriate. I nodded and swallowed a huge lump of fear seasoned with a sense of impending disaster. The man took my keys, and while I watched with the dogs leashed and yelping beside me, he drove my rig out of everyone's way, helped me into the passenger seat and took me to an R.V. repair shop.

The mechanic there explained that I had severed the brake cables between the rig and the vehicle. "It's going to take me at least overnight to repair this thing," he said. "I have to pick up a part."

My new savior smiled at me. "Well," he said. "I guess that means you'll be spending the night with my wife and me. My name is Glen. How do you do?"

"Not very well right now," I said. "My name is Lynn Ruth, but I wouldn't dream of imposing on you that way."

I didn't know this benevolent Galahad and had heard thousands of stories about the dangers of picking up strange men in small towns. Besides, spending the night anywhere involved housing and feeding my three animals. I started to explain my refusal but he silenced me. "I'll just put these little fellers in the back seat, m'am," he said. "You get into the front there and we'll drive over to tell my wife you're coming home with me. She works nights at K-Mart."

The drama of the next few hours happened almost twenty-five years ago but its wonder still amazes me. "I'll have to get some food to take with me, if you really want to take me home. I'm on a restricted salt free diet."

He helped me into his car. "Don't you worry about bringing any food," he said. "You're my guest, tonight," he said. "I'll buy your dinner."

We stopped at K-Mart first to meet his wife. She was a young and very tired woman who was busy checking out items at the front of the store. "This here is Kate," said Glen.

He explained my predicament and Kate smiled at me. "Of course you'll stay with us," she said. "We would just love to have you."

Glen drove me to a grocery store where he bought me the makings of an elaborate dinner. "That is far more than I can eat," I exclaimed and he smiled. "Good," he said. "Then we can send some of the extra home with you. My family doesn't eat this way. We like chicken fried steak and potatoes in our house."

That evening, while dinner was cooking, my benefactor decided to help me shampoo the dogs. He cleaned up the inevitable mess two small children make of a bathroom and dumped the dogs in the bathtub. By the time they were toweled dry, our meal was ready and it was delicious.

He put a mattress on the floor in the master bedroom for his two older children and moved the baby's crib in beside it. He prepared the bed in the other room with clean sheets for me and said good night with the promise, "First thing in the morning we'll get that RV of yours and you'll be on your way."

By eight o'clock the next morning I was on the road again and a man I had only met less than twenty-four hours ago was waving to me as if he had known me all his life. "How can I thank you?" I asked as I settled into the driver's seat.

He blushed. "I don't need no thanks," he said. "I just did what needed to be done."

And indeed he had. He responded to need as automatically as he braked the car for a red light. He thought no more about taking the trouble to help a stranger than he thought about eating breakfast. "I love you," he called as I drove away and I smiled because that was the first time I truly understood the meaning of the phrase. "I love you too!" I called and we both recognized the promise I made to him.

Although I never saw him again, every time I open my heart to a stranger, I am thanking that amazing lover from Winnfield Louisiana. I make his good deed become a pebble in the human stream, sending never-ending ripples of goodness out to the rest of the world.

No act of kindness, however small, is ever wasted
- Aesop

A Merry Christmas

Loneliness is the ultimate poverty
- Abigail van Buren

When I first came to California, I worked for a dating service. I spent a great deal of time searching for just the right companion for my callers but some posed very difficult problems. There was one woman named Gloria who called me from Santa Cruz. I explained that we were required to record a verbal picture of her appearance. "How tall are you?" I asked.

"Five feet, two inches," she said.

"So am I!" I exclaimed. "And what are your proportions?"

"53-30-53," she answered.

"Oh my dear," I said.

John MacDonald also had special needs. He said he sought a compatible personality of any age and I was thrilled. It was particularly difficult to match my upper middle-aged clients and this man sounded ideal. "I have a lot of lovely women for you," I assured him. "Did you want to go out for dinner or dancing?"

"Both," he said. "But afterwards, I'd like to bring them home for a cup of coffee so we can get to know one another."

"I'm sure that will be fine," I said.

"I live in a nudist camp," said John. "My date will have to take off her clothes before I can bring her through the front gate."

"That'll be a challenge," I said.

People who use dating services are usually alone for the holidays so I thought it would be nice to have an open house Christmas day to meet my more difficult patrons. If I actually saw them, perhaps I could do a better job for them.

I decided cake and coffee was the safest thing to serve because I didn't want everyone to get drunk and disturb the neighbors. The obvious dessert was fruitcake. I searched through the cookbooks in the library until I found a recipe that sounded ideal. You poured the batter into coffee cans and added a jigger of rum in them once a week to keep them moist. It was mid December when I started my baking so I decided to double the amount of rum I poured into the cakes and add the alcohol daily. By December 20, I had run out of rum, so I substituted sour mash bourbon I found in the back of my spice cabinet.

By December 23rd, the aroma of the cakes were so strong, I inhaled them in the morning instead of brewing my morning coffee. On Christmas day, I gave the apartment a good cleaning and borrowed a large percolator from my neighbor, Louise. "You come over too," I said. "I'm not doing anything fancy and I'd like you to meet my clients. They are very interesting people."

I hurried back into my kitchen to start the coffee and slice my dessert. To my horror, the cakes were the consistency of a thick pudding. It was too late to substitute anything from the store, so I decided to pour the mixture into sherbet dishes and top each serving with whipped cream. "I can sprinkle them with nutmeg," I told myself. "And put a maraschino cherry on top. They'll be very festive."

My first arrival was Ralph Blackman. He was a mystery to me because he was so charming on the telephone, I couldn't understand how anyone could resist him. He sounded six feet tall and his voice was a very melodic bass. Yet, every partner I found for him refused a second date. He said he drove a red Thunderbird so I knew immediately who he was when he pulled up to the curb. As I watched through the window, a tiny fellow not four feet tall and skinny as a willow skipped out of the car. His cowboy hat was so large it obliterated his face. I opened the door and smiled down at him. "I'm Ralph!" he exclaimed.

"So you are!" I said.

John arrived a few moments later clad in a g-string, thank goodness, and a very snazzy pork pie hat. "Are you sure you won't catch cold?" I asked him. "I keep my thermostat at about 67 degrees."

"Oh, no," he assured me. "But I will keep my hat on. They say you lose most of your body heat through your scalp."

"Would you like some cake?" I asked.

"Would I!" he said. "I haven't eaten a thing all day."

Gloria pulled into my drive in her black Lincoln Continental. She wore a red boucle tee shirt and a green velvet skirt. She sat down on my couch directly under a sprig of mistletoe and smiled at Ralph but he didn't take the hint. Neither did John.

A woman named Valerie Trotter from Santa Rosa was last to arrive. Valerie had refused to go out with John because of her stretch marks and I thought that if they met, chemistry might work in John's favor. He was such a nice person.

My cake was an unbelievable success. Every one of my guests asked for seconds and even thirds and I was delighted. John had consumed five servings of the fruitcake and Gloria was not far behind when Ralph suggested we all sing some Christmas carols. "I'm the choir master at my church," he said. "I'll conduct!"

"If you sing something with a good beat, I'll do my tap dance," said Gloria. "We just had our recital at the Capitola Senior Center and I stole the show."

"What was the song you danced to?" asked John.

"The Burlesque Theater," said Gloria.

"I can play that on my harmonica!" said Ralph.

"I don't know the words but I can do a lovely descant," said Valerie.

"More cake anyone?" I asked.

"Indeed!" shouted my guests.

Just then Louise walked in the door. "I finally made it," she said. "Am I too late for the party?"

"Not at all!" I said. "We were just warming up."

My guests linked arms. "TAKE IT OFF, TAKE IT OFF," they sang.

Gloria swung into a vigorous soft shoe that made the floor heave as if we were having a yuletide earthquake. The others linked arms and roared approval. "This is caroling?" asked Louise.

I looked at the four lonely people gathered in my living room having a marvelous time.

"Not exactly," I said. "But it's certainly Christmas!"

Always pursue pleasure
With breathless haste
- Lynn Ruth

A Mother Knows

Mother's voice clings to my heart
Like trails of bedstraw
That catch you in the lanes
- Mary Webb

Many women have children but only a few are mothers. A true mother always knows everything about you. Absolutely everything.

I had such a mother. I could hide nothing from her. When I walked into the house, my face smeared with chocolate, she would glance at me and say, "How many times do I have to tell you not to eat between meals? No dessert for you, tonight, young lady."

I was shocked. She had been cleaning the bathroom floor while I was at the neighbors pigging out on chocolate cake. How could she see across the street? "How did you know that?" I asked and wiped the crumbs from my chin.

"A mother always knows," she said. "I can read your forehead. Hand me the Bon Ami. I see a finger print on the doorknob."

When I came home from school, my legs twisted into pretzel position and my eyes popping like a choked fish, my mother would point to the bathroom door. "How did you know I had to go?" I asked as I galloped to the toilet.

My mother shrugged. "I read it on your forehead," she explained.

When I got a bit older, her forehead reading became truly remarkable. I could hide absolutely nothing from that woman's penetrating eye. I would come home from a date, my face raw with my escort's affectionate endeavors and my mother would scowl ominously. "Men don't marry fast girls," she announced. "Do you know what time it is?"

"We were only holding hands for God's sake," I lied.

"You can't fool me, Lynn Ruth," said my mother. "I can read the whole vulgar story on your forehead. Put some Jergens on your face or you'll look like a raw tomato tomorrow."

Her amazing knowledge of things she could not see sharpened the farther I was from home. I arrived at college my freshman year, disoriented and lonesome for the very place I had denounced as a suffocating prison hours before. I settled down on the dormitory bed for a good cry when my mother walked in the door. "You forgot your pillow," she said and handed it to me. I had done my own packing and shut the door to my room when we left the house to drive to Ann Arbor. My mother was so nearsighted she couldn't see products on the supermarket shelf without her glasses. How could she possibly make out the print on a forehead sixty miles away?

My mother answered my unspoken question because she could hear it rattling around in my brain. "A mother always knows," she said. "I also brought you some brownies and Rosemary Clooney's latest record release."

"You knew how bad this food is, didn't you?" I said.

"Of course," said my mother.

I was in a violent automobile accident in my late twenties. By that time I had moved out of my mother's house to get a little privacy. My mother who always retired promptly at ten with her potboiler novel and a glass of warm milk, decided to watch the eleven o'clock news. She saw a stretcher move across the screen. The body on it was flat as a pile of magazines except for two tremendous feet protruding through the sheet. My mother sat up and shook my father awake. "Get dressed," she said. "We need to get to the hospital. That's Lynn Ruth."

Time did not diminish my mothers amazing intuition. In fact, it became sharper as I grew older. When I married, she read my impending divorce right through my bridal veil and when I began my job search, she knew the results of my interviews before I received the letters of rejection. When I moved to California in 1980, I was once again victim of a brutal tragedy. I returned from the hospital with stitches in my forehead and legs, two black eyes and bruises all over my body. I staggered into my bedroom and the telephone rang. It was my mother. "Lynn Ruth," she said. "Did you remember tell that doctor you have insurance?"

She knew.

Five years later, my mother succumbed to cancer. Although I called her every night I did not go to visit her until one day, my urge to see her overwhelmed me. I called the airlines and returned home the next day. My mother was on her deathbed. She was so small I could barely locate her among the pillows, sheets and instruments that were keeping her alive. She recognized me at once and held out her wasted arms to embrace me. "Oh, Lynnie," she whispered. "How did you guess how much I wanted you here?"

"I read it on your forehead," I said through my tears.

"In California?" asked my mother.

I realized then that all women have mothers but only a few of them are lucky enough to become daughters, in time. I took my mother's wasted hand in mine. "A daughter always knows," I said.

All women become like their mothers.
- Oscar Wilde

Beautiful Moments

A thing of beauty is a joy forever
- Keats

When I was young, a person's sex determined his expectations and his options in life. Nowadays, women and men have interchangeable roles, wear androgynous costumes and can achieve similar success in any field. There are times of course when it feels great to be feminine and important to be a "man", but these roles are have become choices. I think this is a very good thing.

When I was young, the differences between men and women were absolutes. I was programmed to believe that the amount of glamour I projected was in direct proportion to my success in life. If my entrance into a room did not turn heads and my shape was not the accepted one, I was doomed to a life spent alone.

Men did not have to worry about their appearance. They had other, far more daunting hurdles to overcome. They were expected to be strong, all-knowing and in charge no matter how inadequate they felt inside. "Big Boys Don't Cry" was not a slogan. It was law.

Sometimes, I suppose there is a certain amount of security that stereotypes lend to life, but that kind of consolation has always eluded me. I am not a knock out. I have absolutely no glamour and you know what that means: I am a klutz.

All it takes is one look in the mirror to convince me that my visage is not my strong point. I don't like wasting time on hopeless projects and I get far more positive results when I work packing ideas into my mind. When I graduated with honors from my several colleges, my father patted me on the head and said, "My Lynn Ruth may not be a beauty, but she sure is intelligent."

As I sailed from one career to another, I felt very liberated and independent dressed in no nonsense slacks and sweaters. My face was scrubbed and my attitude direct. Every now and then, I consulted a beauty magazine or entered a beauty salon for serious repair work when I had an interesting date, but these departures from my usual behavior were not only rare, they were unsuccessful.

My mother saw no hope for becoming a grandma much less the mother of a bride. "A man can be one shade uglier than the devil, but a woman must be beautiful," she reminded me every time she saw me in my filthy jeans, dank hair and orthopedic oxfords. "The way you look would not even turn on a radio."

I ignored her. After all, what did she know about living in our modern, liberated world? Her entire life revolved around a stove, a vacuum cleaner and the advice columns in the paper.

And then it happened. One Valentine's Day, an intellectually interesting egghead asked me to marry him and pouf! My attitude did an about face. I became the very stereotype I ridiculed. I dedicated myself to all things feminine. I appeared, professionally coifed wearing bouffant skirts, three inch heels and glimmering jewels for my engagement parties and prepared my body and my weathered face for The Big Moment: my wedding day. For the six months I was engaged, I forgot about being clever. I curtailed all acid repartee and suppressed my churning mind. I had to accomplish a lifetime's worth of skin care, body molding and attitude in just a few months. "Your skin!" groaned the beautician. "It's like shoe leather."

"Your knees!" exclaimed my mother. "Keep them together!"

"Your hair!" they all chorused. "What color IS it?"

I had to exercise to get my middle into the size 6 that was in proportion to my chest; I had to adjust my feet to walking on my toes in high heels and change my skin color from its natural washed sheet tone to peaches and cream. During this time, the only books I read were etiquette books, diet charts, wedding rules and beauty manuals. I knew what perfume to wear when, what nightgowns inspired men to remove them, how to color my lashes so they showed when I batted them and how to keep my lipstick in place when I was crushed in an exciting embrace.

Meanwhile, my prospective groom was playing golf, smoking cigars with the boys and telling nasty jokes in the back room. It was disheartening at best, but after all, that was the way the whole thing was done. Wasn't it?

When the Big Day arrived, I dressed for four hours with my mother and my bridesmaids hovering around me like the experienced coaches they were. I wore an elaborate, satin dress with an immense train that trailed behind me. My hair had been sprayed to the consistency of cotton candy even a cyclone could not disturb. My face was covered with creams, subtle colors and concealers to create the illusion of natural beauty and even my underwear was fit for royalty to view.

My father met me at the entrance to the temple and together we walked down the aisle to meet the man I would marry. Heads turned, I heard gasps of admiration and all the elderly women wept into their lace handkerchiefs.

My husband-to-be smiled at me, and I could see the amazement in his eyes. He took me in his arms after I had actually committed myself to honor and obey him and whispered, "I have never seen you look so beautiful."

I am ashamed to admit that I was thrilled.

Within weeks, I came to terms with the grim reality of filthy toilets, shaving cream in the sink and piles of dishes insisting I address them before the rats did. I realized that I could not orchestrate my appearance, when the guy was standing right there pushing me aside to adjust his tie. I stopped being glamorous and resumed being me. The marriage managed to struggle though a couple agonized years of disillusion and now I am once more engaged in my comfortable, slovenly gallop through life. I am no longer into skirts. I put nothing on my face but soap. Indeed, I am back to the no-frills lifestyle I do best and I usually have no regrets.

After all, everyone knows a person's face isn't his beauty. It is his spirit. All human beings are exquisite when they open their hearts to one another. And yet . . . and yet . . . When life deals a body blow to my ego and my glorious dreams shatter, it is always nice to close my eyes and remember that magic day when I was the moment and it was beautiful.

The richness of life lies in memories . . .
- Pavese

The Beauty That Endures

Does one get wise as time passes on,
Or is it only that one's old folly goes out of fashion?
- Geraldine Endsor

I re-educated late in life and after I graduated, I began a job search. For three endless years, I answered ads from coast to coast, but, although I filled out countless applications, I had no offers at all. My father said it was because I am a woman and a middle-aged one at that. "That idea went out with the Charleston," I told him. "A woman can do anything a man can nowadays."

"I wonder," said my father.

My mother insisted it was because I have no style and I knew she was right. Oh, I'm clean and neat enough, but I don't spend a lot of time in dress stores and beauty shops. Still, I dismissed both my parents' reasons as foolish and superficial. "People aren't hired by their looks," I said. "If I had the right qualifications, an employer wouldn't care if I dressed in a burlap bag and had eyes in the back of my head."

I believe this because I think that way. I value people because of their goodness and I measure their worth by their capabilities. I assumed that was how others judged me. And so I ignored my parents' pessimism and concentrated on polishing my writing skills so that when opportunity knocked, I would be ready to open the door.

At last, I received a telephone call inviting me to Madison, Wisconsin to be interviewed for a writing position. The personnel director of the newspaper there explained that it would take about two days for me to meet the managing editor, the department heads and the people I might be working with. "How soon can you get here?" he asked.

I could hardly contain my excitement. The work he described was the kind I had always dreamed of doing. I knew I could handle the job. Better, I knew I would love every minute of it. "I'll be there tomorrow," I said.

The next morning, I closed my house and hurried to the airport. I bubbled excitement as I chattered to everyone I saw. The flight was filled with interesting people with a lot to say, and I had a wonderful time.

The personnel director met me at the airport and drove me to the executive offices of the newspaper. He ushered me into a plush, well-appointed office. "Mr. Garfield will be right in to meet you," he said.

In just a few moments, the door burst open and the managing editor walked in. He introduced himself and began talking immediately about the tremendous employee turnover he had at his newspaper. "I really can't understand it," he said. "We pay very good salaries here, and our fringe benefits are unequalled anywhere in the state. I guess it's the kind of people who seek employment these days. They just aren't stable; they take no pride in their work."

As he talked, he paced the floor and smoked one cigarette after another. Abruptly, he walked to the door. "I must leave. I have a deadline in just half an hour."

And he was gone.

I had not said one single word.

In a few moments, the personnel director returned. "Well, you can go home now," he said.

"You mean that's all?" I asked. "Isn't anyone going to ask me any questions? Aren't I going to meet any of the editors?"

"Mr. Garfield doesn't feel you would fit in with us here," he answered. "He has a sixth sense about these things."

He drove me to the airport and booked me for the evening plane. As I sat in the airport, the full impact of what had happened hit me. I had been rejected for the way I looked - nothing more. I went to the mirror in the Ladies Room and peered at my reflection. For the first time, I saw me. I looked at a plain, middle-aged woman with lines around her eyes from years of laughter and wrinkles on her forehead from years of worry.

And then I cried. I cried tears of frustration because I had been judged for something I could not help, for something that told no more about my writing ability than an orange peel tells how sweet the fruit will taste. I cried tears of fury because it was so very unfair to dispose of me like an unwanted piece of paper. And then I cried tears of humiliation. My parents were right after all and I had been so sure they were not.

I was very quiet on the trip home. I did not talk to my fellow passengers for fear I would repel them. I drove home from the airport overwhelmed with somber thoughts of a future without hope. But when I opened the door of my house, I was warmed by the sight and smell of so much that was familiar to me, and I smiled once more. I felt once again that I belonged somewhere, that I had a place to love and be loved.

From that moment on, I wasted no more tears on the things about me that I could not change. Instead, I thought of that man and all the people like him in this world that base their judgments on the color of someone's skin or the curl of his hair. How tenuous it must seem to build your every hope on foundations as fragile as a passing fad, as evanescent as a rainbow. As I stood in the welcome comfort of my own solid world, I again saw that nervous, pacing man, and I cried once more.

But this time, I cried for him.

Beauty is all very well at first sight;
But who ever looks at it
When it has been in the house three days?
- G. B. Shaw

Being Daddy

It is a wise father that knows his own child.
- Shakespeare

When I was a child, I envied Normie Odesky because her father took her with him to basketball games, football rallies and wrestling matches even when her mother had to stay at home to clean the house. It never occurred to me that Mr. Odesky was using his daughter as an excuse to go to these events. I thought he was being a very nice daddy.

Sometimes the Odeskys invited me to join them and even though I had no interest in sports, I loved being with them because they had so much fun together. Mr. Odesky was Normie's best friend and I thought that must be a very wonderful thing for her.

I hardly knew my daddy. My father had ulcers and because he was always in great pain, our household revolved around his special needs. He was a quiet man and even though we rarely had a conversation, I sensed a gentleness about him that made me love him very much. I was pretty sure that affection wasn't returned because my father was little more than a shadowy presence in our family. He paid as little attention to us as possible and when he saw my sister and me, he couldn't even remember our names. He called my sister "The Baby" and he would pause when he addressed me and then call me "Princess". I knew he always remembered my mother's name because he said "Ida. Can't you keep those kids quiet?" at least twice a day.

In the forties, a girl's sixteenth birthday was considered her passage into the adult world. Most of my friends were given big parties on that day and Normie Odesky's daddy took her to the Kin Wa Lo Nightclub to celebrate. Normie got to wear high-heeled shoes and nylon stockings and she even put on real lipstick instead of Tangee Natural. "They served me a Shirley Temple Cocktail and a comedian told a lot of off-color stories," she told me.

"How wonderful!" I said and turned my face away so she couldn't see the tears gathering in my eyes.

There would be no party for me on my sixteenth birthday. My father had scheduled major surgery the first week in October and my mother warned me that she would have to stay at his bedside on my big day. I came downstairs to breakfast on October 11th and there was no gift waiting for me; not even a card tucked under my plate. My mother was on her way out the door. "They finally took all the tubes out of Daddy," she said. "He ate his first solid food last night!"

"Does that mean he can come home soon?" I asked.

My mother nodded. "The doctor said next week for sure. Your orange juice is on the counter and there are some cinnamon rolls left over from yesterday in the bread box," she said.

I watched her leave the house without saying so much as "happy birthday" to me, but before I my tears had a chance to fall, my favorite cousin Murray called to ask me out for dinner. "I just realized this is your sixteenth birthday, Lynn Ruth!" he said. "Do you think you could stand going out for dinner at the Hillcrest with an old man like me?"

"Oh wow! Could I!" I exclaimed and then I remembered that I was sixteen and no longer a child. I cleared my throat. "How lovely of you to remember me!"

Well, I don't know how thrilled Normie Odesky was when she went to that nightclub but I do know that I could barely sit still with anticipation for my dinner date with a twenty year old man. This was maturity!

Murray picked me up at six that night and we drove downtown in his yellow Ford convertible. My cousin took my hand and led me to the elevator. "The dining room is in there," I said and I pointed to the large area on the other side of the door. "I've ordered a very special dinner for your birthday, Lynnie Ruth," said Murray. "It's upstairs in the Tower Room."

I could hardly believe his words. The Tower Room was where people held wedding parties and magnificent receptions. "How neat!" I breathed.

When the elevator opened, and we entered the Tower Room, there was Normie Odesky and all my friends waving banners and balloons. "HAPPY BIRTHDAY, LYNNIE RUTH!" they said and I began to cry. I thought the only special gift I would receive was a leftover cinnamon roll for breakfast and instead I got my very first birthday party with every single person I loved right there to celebrate with me. Everyone that is, except my parents. "Did you plan this?" I said to Murray and he shook his head. "Your mother knew she wouldn't be able to celebrate your birthday tonight," he explained. "And so she arranged this big surprise party instead."

I thought of my worried mother taking time away from helping my sick father to create a spectacular event for me and I began to cry again. "I never thought she would bother to do something so nice for me," I sobbed.

Murray took my hand. "Well, that's your second surprise, tonight. Let's have dinner."

Well, the meal was delicious and I blew out all seventeen candles on an immense chocolate cake. "What did you wish for?" asked Murray

"I wished that my daddy would get well," I said.

The band began to play "Deep Purple" and Murray smiled. "Let's dance," he said.

We walked to the dance floor and Murray nodded toward the door. My father had just entered the room and was walking toward us. He was stooped over a little and he looked very pale. He took my hand and he kissed me. "Happy Birthday, Princess," he said. "May I have this dance?"

There is always one remembered moment
When "father" becomes another name for love.
- Lynn Ruth

Being Mother

Once upon a time, wife and servant were synonyms.
- Lynn Ruth a la Lady Mary Chudleigh

In the days that some fools still insist were good, my grandmother labored from six in the morning until midnight scrubbing floors, washing windows, doing laundry, cooking endless meals from scratch, sewing clothes, stretching her husband's income to feed a growing family, monitoring the behavior of her children and nurturing their minds. At night, after the children were in bed, the mending done, the clothes ironed and the house put in order, she retired with my grandfather to create still another child.

My grandma had no time to worry about what she wore or how she was entertained. She was lucky if she found a moment to go to the bathroom. Dust and dishes never stop gathering and little children always need.

There are women who thrive in that kind of regime and my grandma was one. She was a happy, loving woman. She was also uneducated. She had no idea that there was a world beyond her front porch and her greatest satisfaction was the roof over her head. Her next blessing was her first-born daughter with red hair, blue eyes and an American future. There were other children and other rewards but I doubt that my grandfather was one of them. He was a surly man who came home each night after a long day of plastering other people's walls, sat down without a word and waited until my grandma served him the meal she had managed to create from the few coins he allowed her each week.

My mother was determined not to become a victim of the slavery she saw in the home my grandfather built for his Romanian bride. She was certain the key that would open the door to comfort and security was hidden in her husband's income. She determined to marry a professional man who could erase the humiliation of a barren childhood with never enough to eat and one dress worn until it was in shreds. My mother wanted a home in a nice neighborhood, fashion in her closet, beauticians to pamper her and travel to amuse her. She sought maids to clean and iron and a well-behaved child to show off to the world. She endured the birthing process because it would reward her with a little puppet that accomplished all the things she hadn't managed to achieve.

However, when I was born, my mother didn't get the pleasure she anticipated. She hadn't realized that a child is not a piece of clay. She didn't remember that no one molded her into anything she didn't choose. My mother was impatient for the good things of life. It took my father many years to build up enough resources to give her the lifestyle she wanted. Meanwhile, she was faced with a little dreamer who didn't wear clothes well and lost herself in the pages of a book.

How could she escape? Her high school education didn't prepare her to support herself, not did it give her resources to build something different. She did not live in a cosmopolitan place where opportunities were a subway ride away. She was stuck in Toledo, Ohio with a drudge for a husband and a child who couldn't do anything right. A cruel fate had made her a mother just like the one she had escaped while her bed partner worked ten to twelve hours seven days a week to support them both. Motherhood finished any hope she had for escape and she never hid her anger from me

My mother was an angry, unhappy woman, but my grandma was not and it was she who nourished me. She and I sang and laughed whenever we were together because we were in love.

My mother hated the ethnic meals my grandma prepared, rich with starch and void of imagination. She fed me nutritionally balanced meals with no dessert until I ate my spinach. I became a sallow skinny child who never grew tall. The minute I walked into my grandma's house, my cheeks became roses and my ebullience bubbled like champagne. Any food she set before me was heaven. "Eat, Leenie Rute," she would say and I gobbled up corned beef laced with garlic, soup so greasy that looking at it put a shine on my nose and slice after slice of rye bread drenched in sweet butter. I don't believe there was anyone in my life I adored as much as I did that tiny woman who smelled like starched clothes and a bakery. I was certain that she was God.

But she was not any such thing. She was a woman who did not know her human potential. She could have painted pictures and written books. She could have heard a symphony or seen a play. She could have shared her wisdom with a humanity starving for the kind of faith and optimism she poured into the one person who heard her. She was perfection to me, but she could have been so much more.

And so could my mother. My mother only saw the trap woman stepped in when they said "I Do." She didn't know that there were books to teach her and a wealth of creative outlets for those frustrations of hers. She didn't have college. She didn't have awareness groups and television specials. She had never tried to tap the immense gold in her imagination. Although she saw her mother's happiness, she never managed to figure out how it happened.

These days, we have the right to express ourselves and the knowledge of how to do it. We have options. Today's mother can be a woman who juggles her own needs with her obligations and creates challenging patterns for her children to see in action. If they hear other tunes to the music of life, today's mothers need not be afraid to let them dance their own way. I thank heaven that no woman need be a stereotype, today. She can become herself.

We are such stuff as dreams are made on.
- Shakespeare

Being Sandy

Oh, the comfort- the inexpressible comfort
Of feeling safe with a person
- George Eliot

When my mother was angry with me, she would look at me as if I were a malevolent piece of litter and shout, "Why can't you be like Sandy?"

Sandy was my second cousin and the child of my mother's best friend since childhood, my Aunt Sally. As far as my mother was concerned, Aunt Sally was consistently showered with the gold of life and my mother had to settle for dross. Her marriage lacked passion, her economic situation was tight and (the final blow), her daughter was an awkward clunk with absolutely no ability in anything that mattered.

Sandy was a well-proportioned blonde child, so obedient she went to bed promptly at seven, brushed her teeth ALWAYS and never sucked her thumb. She sat at the table with her hand in her lap and never spilled a single crumb on the tablecloth. This model child (according to Aunt Sally) always ate everything on her plate, including spinach and liver and never ever smeared chocolate pudding on her face. Her teeth appeared right on time, she was toilet trained in moments after birth and her bowel habits were more reliable than sunrise and sunset.

On the other hand, I was dark and awkward. I had black circles under my eyes from trying to read after the light had been turned out and my hair hung like limp string. I had skinny legs and enormous feet and although I did indeed brush my teeth, I did a lousy job. I, too, kept my hand in my lap, but I never ate anything at all because I was desperately afraid that I would say something to make my mother angry. My stomach throbbed and battled anything I put in it and it was rare that I could sit through an entire meal without giving most of it back to the plumbing system (If I managed to get there in time). To make matters worse, I never drank my milk, refused my spinach and what with all the tension in my house, I set records for chronic constipation.

My cousin Sandy was beautifully coordinated from birth (according to my Aunt Sally). She could ride a two wheeled bicycle at two, she skipped rope with no problem the moment she learned to walk which was six months before any other child in recorded medical history. When she played outdoors, she returned (the moment her mother called her, of course) without a smudge on her pinafore or a curl (natural) out of place. She was brilliant in kindergarten, stunning all her teachers with her verbal ability and dexterity and graceful in dance class. A delightful child!

Each time my mother forced me outside to play, I stood at the back door begging to return to my books and my teddy bear. My mother would hand me a yoyo and say, “Play with that, Lynn Ruth,” and I, petrified to incur any more wrath than my very existence created for her, would attempt to make the elusive cylinder climb back up its rope. I spent most of my time outdoors sitting on the back step rewinding my yoyo, weeping and shivering until the call came for me to return to my home. If I was brave enough to venture forth into the jungle that was Islington Street, I inevitably fell and skinned my knee before I got past our driveway. I tried to skip rope several times only to land on the cement. Hopscotch was as horrifying to me as doing a balance act on the telephone wires above my house. I can still remember the terror that paralyzed me when my father tried to teach me to ride a two-wheeled bicycle. It was only surpassed by the panic that choked me when he forced me to sit behind the wheel of an automobile.

My mother enrolled me in Patricia Heineman’s dance class when I was four years old and I had such a terrible time getting my feet into my tap shoes that the half hour was almost over before I managed to stand in the line to mangle even one hop, brush, brush, tap, tap. When my mother came to pick me up, she had long whispered discussions with Miss Heineman and as soon as she hauled me into the car she would turn on me with disgust and say, ”Why can’t you be like Sandy? Aunt Sally says she’ll be in toe shoes by next week and she’s only been taking ballet for two weeks. She graduated from tap when she was three, for God’s sake.”

I clutched my teddy bear to my empty heart and I, too, wished I could be like Sandy. I liked my cousin Sandy. She was a dear good friend to me and never failed to say something encouraging to me even after my mother pointed out how adorable she looked in her clothes and how gracefully she walked with her toes pointing straight ahead instead of east and west as mine always did. Sandy had the kind of presence a child develops when she and her mother are good friends. She knew how valuable she was and since that issue was settled, all she had to do was be herself. I was so certain I should take up residence in the nearest dumpster, that my every effort was devoted to convincing everyone else of a value I didn’t believe I had.

I never realized that Sandy’s magic made everyone close to her go through a stage when they want to be just like her until I visited her many years later when she was married to a lovely man who washed windows and had two adorable babies of her own. By that time, I had divorced a realistic man who didn't like me any better than my mother did, and had no children to show for the life I had lived on earth. I looked at Sandy's beautiful home and gorgeous children and knew this wasn't ever to be in my future. By that time I was old enough and wise enough to know that I needed to be like Lynn Ruth if I wanted to experience any kind of success with my life.

Sandy cooked us all a magnificent dinner with so little effort I could hardly believe everything tasted as delicious as it did and after we put the girls to bed, we stayed up to talk. There was never a time in my life when talking to Sandy didn't make me happy to be me and that evening was no exception. She admired all the things in me that always infuriated my mother. Believe me, receiving compliments from the person I had tried for so many years to emulate was honey filled confection for me. To Sandy, my stellar characteristic was my 20/20 vision. My cousin had to wear glasses from the time she was a very small child and the moment contact lenses came on the market, she got them and wore them always.

After hours of good conversation, the two of us went to bed and the next morning we both went into the children's' bedroom to say good morning to them. There was Stephanie sitting on the bed with Jody. "Lets play house," said Jody.

"All right," said Stephanie. "I'll be the mommy."

She sat up in bed, groped on the bedside table and leaned over to put an imaginary something in each eye. I turned to my cousin. "What is she doing?" I asked and Sandy laughed.

"She's putting in her contacts," she said. "She's trying to be me."

I nodded. "It's a stage," I said. "I went through it myself."

Years have passed since that time. Both Sandy and I have come to terms with what we are and I feel sure her three daughters have done the same. But it is always nice to remind someone as special as Sandy that she is so inspiring that all of us who love her want to be just like her at one point in our lives. That period of time is the hiatus we all need to gather the strength to become ourselves.

Our hearts are always warm in your presence
- Lynn Ruth and Lady Mary Montague

Creating Spring

There is no reality
except the one contained within us.
- Hermann Hesse

In Toledo, Ohio, spring is a mirage always anticipated but seldom seen. Winter 's icy grasp paralyzes the place well into May when one prayed for evening, somewhere near May 31st, the temperature zooms from ten below zero to ninety degrees, with 110% humidity. In March of the year I was teaching Art Appreciation at the university there, winter was beginning to seem eternal. I left for work at six a.m. bundled up in several layers of thermal underwear, three heavy sweaters, fleece lined leggings, an insulated storm coat, two heavy scarves and waterproof mittens over my fleece lined gloves. I wedged myself behind the steering wheel of my Renault and managed to get the engine sufficiently thawed to turn over by seven thirty. If there were no collisions on the highway and luck was with me, I covered the five miles to the school, my bladder bursting and my nerves destroyed, just in time for my three o'clock class.

I sloshed into my classroom where my students were huddled around the heat vent to launch a unit on the painters of the Renaissance. "Good Morning!" I cried. "Today, we will discuss La Primavera."

The group took their seats, opened their notebooks and looked at me expectantly. "What is La Primavera?" asked Harvey, his voice muffled by scarves and sweaters.

"Our assignment," I said.

"My question was not about the painting," he said. "It was about the title. What does it mean?"

"Spring." I said.

My class looked at me as if I had uttered an obscenity. "What is spring?" asked Mary Pat. "I've never seen it."

"Yes you have," said Jonathan. "Don't you remember 1961? It was 50 degrees in April."

"Was that the year the floods swept away Superior Street?"

I propped a large reproduction of the Botticelli masterpiece on the chalk tray and tapped my desk for attention. "Let us discuss this painting, please," I said. """What are the characters doing here?"

My class gazed at the cluster of nymphs, and maidens, ready targets for a naked Cupid. "They are dancing with joy and chasing after one another with pagan lust," said Laura.

"Obviously, Botticelli has never experienced Midwestern weather," said Harvey. "None of us have ever seen a season like this. Any fool who attempts to satisfy his lust in March around here, would be frozen into position until June."

"That is a coarse way to put it," I said.

"Truth is truth," observed Harvey."

"Nature is doing the best she can," I said. "It is up to us to encourage her efforts using the power of our minds. If every one of us in this room thought spring, that's what it would become. Haven't you ever heard that saying, 'Nothing's either good or bad but thinking makes it so'?"

"That's just what it is," said Mary Pat. "A saying. "

"Only if you think so," I said with what I hoped was a wise smile. "If we create a tableau of Botticelli's painting on the front lawn, we could actually transform the climate around us."

"Impossible," said Harvey. "If forced air heat can't get the temperature up to seventy degrees, our tableau won't stand a chance."

"I don't know about that," said Mary Pat. "I remember once when I thought I was sure a truck was going to ram right into my car. I closed my eyes and willed it to swerve to the left."

"And did it?" asked Laura.

Mary Pat nodded. "Yes, it did. It rammed into a little pink Volkswagen trying to pass me on the right."

Phillip Spitzer was my very favorite student. His was the kind of optimism I thought had gone out of style in the younger generation and every time he answered my questions with his sunny smile and inspiring positive attitude, I understood why I so loved my teaching career. "I'll bet you fifty bucks that we can create spring out there," he said to Harvey.

"You're on," said Harvey.

We all chose parts in the painting and decided to stage our tableau at our meeting the following day. "I'm going to invite Dean Rochte to see this," I said. "We will amaze him."

The next day at three, all of us gathered on the front steps of the Humanities Building, dressed in filmy gowns and stadium boots. "The weather forecast said blizzard conditions," said Harvey. "I hope you have your fifty dollars ready, Phillip. I don't accept I.O.U.'s."

"Positions!" I called and my students assembled into their assigned poses. Kendall waved a tree branch menacingly at the gathering clouds and Mary Pat scattered Burpee seed packets across the frosted lawn. Phillip stood on a statue of William Perry in floral boxer shorts with a bow and arrow in his hand and aimed it at Laura. Laura looked up at him and leered. "You have adorable legs but they are very bristly," she observed.

"Those are goose bumps," said Phillip. "Watch out. I am going to shoot!"

His arrow flew through the air and landed in the oak tree at the foot of the steps. As I stared at my group, their teeth chattering and their hair tousled by gusts of wind, the sun pushed aside the gray clouds and burst upon our masterpiece. The air was suffused with sweet floral perfume and the trees seemed to burst into leaf. The dean came hurrying across the lawn unbuttoning his coat. He gazed up at the blazing sun and then at the tableau my students had created and shook his head. "Amazing!" he said. "That's spring! How did you do it?"

"We used the power of our minds," I said "Isn't that what college is for?"

"Look!" exclaimed Laura. "I found a whole cluster of violets!"

"You owe me fifty bucks, Harvey," said Phillip.

I examined the violets Laura held more closely. There was a tag on it that said, "Grown with love by Feniger's Flowers."

Laura's eyes met mine. "My mom always said that flower shop created miracles," she said.

"How do you plan to spend that fifty, Phillip?" I asked.

Phillip grinned. "To buy us all hot fudge sundaes!" he said.

"I think I'm in love with you!" I said. "Do you suppose my fancy has turned at last?"

"You're probably hungry," said Laura. "It's almost five."

"Shall we dance?" said Kendall and he gave me his arm.

"But there's no music!" said Mary Pat.

"Oh yes there is," said Phillip. "Listen! That's Mendelssohn's Spring Symphony!"

"There's a robin!" cried Laura. "It really is spring."

Kendall took me in his arms and I whispered, "Where did you hide the tape recorder?"

"Behind that dumpster where Laura put the empty florist box."

I smiled up at him. "You do a mean waltz."

"That's because it's spring," said Kendal and we whirled across the greening lawn.

Experience is not what happens to a man;
It is what a man does with what happens to him.
- Aldous Huxley

Daily Valentines

We're made kind by being kind
- Eric Hoffer

The most lasting acts of love are often unnoticed because they are done with so little fanfare. They are daily occurrences inspired by a generous heart. All of us have been the recipients of these unexpected and magnificent deeds. Once received, they flower into memories that deepen throughout our lives. I cherish all these gifts of the heart and recall them with warmth long after I receive them. But one I received from a ten-year-old child has never been equaled for me.

In the fifties, I tutored a developmentally disabled child named Debby Ware. Her mother scheduled a conference with me and as we spoke, I realized she thought her daughter lacked every mental and social skill that created a functioning human being. "I have been taking her to tutors ever since she was five years old," said Mrs. Ware. "But she is so thick, nothing penetrates. Thank God it isn't hereditary. Her two brothers are A students and star athletes. Debby is ten years old and cannot even set the table. All she does is daydream and hum little songs to herself. Can you believe that?"

Indeed I could believe it. I too could never remember on which side to put the fork or where to place a water glass. I was wrapped up in romantic notions about the prince awakening Sleeping Beauty and worried lest that little frog would never stop spitting diamonds and get a life.

I fully expected to greet a drooling dunce when Debby knocked on my classroom door the next day. Instead, I met a serious little girl, gentle and refreshing as cool water on the desert. She had an aura of simplicity about her so charming that I felt enriched just sitting beside her. We bonded immediately and I adored her. I found her neither backward nor poorly coordinated. She was not an impulsive child. Instead she addressed every problem with slow careful precision. It was apparent that her qualities were not the intellectual or physical ones prized in her home and at school. They were gifts of the spirit. Debby thrilled to the shine of the sun and the song of a bird. One could kindle her laughter with a hug and thrill her with her favorite cookie or cobweb on the windowpane.

We met three times a week and together we translated the hieroglyphics on a page into something meaningful for her. Debby learned to read with me even though she may not have enjoyed the process. For over a year, she appeared on time for every lesson and never moved from her chair beside my desk until I hugged her and said." Good job, Debby! See you day after tomorrow."

She stood up and smiled at me as if I had told her she had won a Nobel Prize. I helped her with her coat and took her hand. "Let's wait outside for your mother, Debby," I said and we walked to front of the building. Mrs. Ware pulled up to the curb, honked the horn and Debby would squeeze my hand and tilt her cheek for my good-bye kiss. As they drove away, Debby leaned out the window to wave until the car turned the corner.

The following year, we continued her lessons, but one month into the term, I was in an almost fatal automobile accident. My eyes loosened from their sockets, my foot and arm were broken and the left side of my face had to be rebuilt. I was swathed in bandages and walked with a crutch. Although I could not resume classroom teaching, Mrs. Ware called and asked if I would continue tutoring Debby. "She is having a terrible time in the fourth grade," she said. "She never would have passed out of the third without you and now I'm afraid they'll put her back there again."

"I would love to help Debby," I said. "But she might be frightened when she sees me. My face is covered with dressings and my arm is in a cast."

"Debby wouldn't care if you were a mummy chained to a casket," said Mrs. Ware. "She asks when she can see you every day."

And so once again, three times a week, Mrs. Ware drove her child to me, this time in my mother's house. She walked down the hall to my room and set her books down on my desk. She never reacted to the bandages, the cast, and my muffled speech. She sat with her hand in her lap while I found the correct page and began to explain the words and what they meant. We concentrated as hard as we could for thirty minutes and then we drew pictures and talked about what Debby did when she not with me. She had no friends that were important to her and her conversation revolved around all the wonderful things her brothers were allowed to do. "Someday, maybe I can learn to ride a bicycle too," she said. "Then Daddy will buy me a red one just like Robert has."

At four o'clock, Mrs. Ware pulled into our driveway and honked the horn. Debbie put away our crayons and paper, closed her book. "Good-bye, Miss Miller," she said and tilted her cheek for my kiss. I stood at the door just as I had stood in front of the school and watched her hurry into her mother's waiting car. She waved to me once more before the two of them drove away.

Debby 's love for me was so strong, I still feel its comfort. She showed me her devotion when she placed a pencil in my bandaged hand, when she opened the door so I could limp into our study room, when she looked into my mangled face and glowed with pleasure at the me behind them. I was her teacher and I was beautiful to her.

I may have taught Debby to read, but she taught me something far more important. She taught me that love makes all things possible. If the teachers she had met before me had bothered to work with the child instead of a printed page, Debby Ware would have been reading long before she was ten years old. If Mrs. Ware had taken the time to notice how many special qualities her child possessed, she might have valued her little girl's achievements as much if not more than her sons' prowess with a baseball bat and a scholastic achievement test. Debby was skilled in seeing beauty in a raindrop or a haunting melody. She could thrill at a rainbow and weep at a puppy's kiss. Whenever it is time to send or receive valentines, I remember my magic student and I know how fortunate I was to receive her brilliantly shining valentine every day for three years, a valentine that never diminished in its intensity. Her gift of love lives within me and never stops enriching me. What better valentine can there be?

Love believes all things, hopes all things
And endures all things
- Corinthians

Determination

Music expresses that which is inexpressible
- Aldous Huxley

My Aunt Tick had a canary that loved to sing to the motor of her vacuum cleaner. The roar of that machine filled the bird's heart with musical inspiration and he responded with counter melodies that trilled high above the whoosh of sucked up litter and demolished trash.

He demonstrated his single-minded devotion to his art one unforgettable day when my aunt decided to clean her draperies. As she hauled out the vacuum cleaner and attached the extension hose, the bird's delight was actually visible. He knew that soon he would have a well-deserved orchestral accompaniment for his opera grande and he was right. My aunt turned on the machine and the little golden bird responded with a sublime Missa Gloria. Aunt Tick was so involved with her task that she didn't notice that her pet warbler had emerged from his cage and let the force of his melody sweep him to the top of the cornice.

The cleaner blared and the melodious canary launched into yet another aria inspired by the angels. As my aunt lifted the vacuum cleaner wand to get into the drapery folds, she saw a flash of yellow disappear down the vacuum cleaner tube. She was horrified.

She switched off the machine, certain her poor bird had left the earth for a heavenly choir and then she paused. The bird's song was clear as a celestial hymn sung from a distant loft. "Keep singing, darling!" called Aunt Tick. "Mama will save you!"

She unzipped the bag and now the bird's voice was sweet and very clear. My distraught aunt burrowed deep into the dust bunnies and crumbled tissue until at last; she cleared a pathway for her operatic pet to escape. The bird shot from the bag like a released bullet and landed on the coffee table still singing the main motif of his Vacuum Symphony.

My aunt stared at her pet with renewed respect. The canary was perched on an ashtray without a single feather left on his body. He was pink and naked as the day he was hatched, his tiny throat still vibrating with song.

When I picture that little bird proclaiming his joie de vivre to the world despite all odds, I wonder if the human race could equal such dedication. Would Pavarotti have continued his aria if he'd lost his pants? Would Carol

Vanes have sung her golden notes if her bra strap broke? Indeed not. But nothing could stop my aunt's canary from singing his glorious song. Nothing.

And so whenever I remember that joyous canary, I resolve to sing my own song loud and clear despite the obstacles that threaten to silence me. It is, after all, the most precious thing I can give to the world. It is my gift.

One can never consent to creep
When he feels the need to soar.
- Helen Keller

Farewell to the Tooth Fairy

We are so constituted that we
believe the most incredible things
- Goethe

When we are children, fantasy is a comforting thing and as I was growing up, I retreated into that world often to escape from an unbending reality. When I was forced to take a nap, I would cover my head with a blanket and make up tales of worlds where mothers didn't scream and you could eat all the ice cream you could hold. I wished upon every star and when I blew out the candles on my birthday cake, I sent up endless pleas for new puppies, picture books or permission to sleep at Marcia Zimmerman's because her mother made blueberry waffles for breakfast.

It wasn't until I was nine years old that my comforting fantasies were taken from me and I felt as wounded as if I had been shot. World War II had been raging for almost two years and we were learning to live with rationed gasoline, meatless Tuesdays and endless paper drives. Each time I lost a tooth, I would place it under my pillow, confident that the next morning, the tooth fairy would replace it with a dime to spend any way I pleased.

When I was nine, I was losing molars and sometimes it was difficult to pull them without a twinge of pain. When my Mama tied a string around the tooth and pulled with all her might, I endured without a sound because I knew of the reward to come. You could buy a whole box of cracker jacks with a dime and get a special prize at the bottom of the box. You could purchase a yo-yo and even a double dip ice cream cone and you didn't even have to ask permission.

The night after I had pulled out my first molar, I was awakened by a slight rustle at my bedroom door. When I opened my eyes, I saw Daddy rummaging under my pillow to replace my tooth with a coin. Copper had become so scarce that our government substituted aluminum in pennies that year and because the light was dim and my father was tired, I got one cent instead of ten. I discovered his error as soon as he left the room and I was inconsolable.

I came downstairs to breakfast the next morning, barely able to suppress my tears. I put the penny on the sink and said, "Why did you tell me the tooth fairy rewarded me for a lost tooth when you knew all along that it wasn't true?"

My mother put her arm around my shoulder and made me sit down with her at the kitchen table. "It is people in this world who make magic things happen," she explained. "And I am going to tell you about a lady you know who has done that very thing. Do you remember Aunt Bess Terman?"

I nodded and my mother told me about the many years my Aunt Bess had prayed and prayed for a child but never got one. By the time she and Uncle Max tried to adopt a baby, they were so old, that social service agencies wouldn't consider their application. My Aunt Bess did volunteer work at a children's hospital and one day she saw a little boy so malnourished he could barely move. He was being fed through tubes and one of the nurses pointed to the wasted child. "That youngster won't last a month and there's nothing really wrong with him. He was starved for days when the police found him crammed into the trunk of a car," she explained. "But he is so frightened that he refuses to eat and screams all through the night."

Aunt Bess walked over to this little boy's bed and she put her hand on his head. As she stroked his bright curly hair she could feel the child quiver and she saw his eyes dart back and forth like a hunted animal. She picked him up, tubes and all and held him to her breast. "I'll take him," she said. "I'll make him well."

In those days, you could do a thing like that without signing endless papers. Within an hour, Aunt Bess became the temporary guardian of that little boy. She wrapped him in a blanket and brought him home. She named him Bernard.

In the beginning, she fed him with a spoon and an eyedropper and she stayed at his bedside all night so he would never awake to find himself alone. She listened to his nightmares and she comforted him. She walked him around the block as slowly as if they were both crippled and by the time I became aware of Bernie Terman, he was a skinny little boy who loved to laugh and play hop scotch with all of us on the block. "Bess did a magic thing," said my mother. "She saved that little child with love alone. When your father came into your room last night, he was not letting you believe a lie. He was showing you that magic is the power real people have to make a better world."

I pushed my spoon around my rice krispies and I swallowed very hard. "I suppose you're going to tell me there is no magic elf in this cereal that goes snap, crackle and pop and no soap fairy to make Ivory float."

My mother nodded. "It's all in how you look at it," she said. "A human being thought of a way to let your bath bar float in the tub and make your cereal dance for you. Those are the good fairies in a real world. Can you understand that?"

I nodded. "Yes, I can," I said, "But what I can't figure out is who owes me nine cents."

The truth is the hardest missile
one can be pelted with
- George Eliot

Hot Gospel

One touch of nature makes the whole world kin
- Shakespeare

You do not know what a real heat wave is until you have been in Texas in August. I was living in a fifth wheel trailer in the Texas Hill Country the summer of 1980 when it was 110 degrees at night. I shared my residence with 2 dogs: Molly a bilious mutt who loved to kiss, Cindy an elitist poodle, an independent cat, Eileen and no air conditioning. I woke up each morning par boiled. By sunset, I was medium rare and ran the risk of being consumed by anyone with cannibalistic tendencies.

Each morning I filled a percolator with the water heating in my holding tank and put it on the front step to percolate while I placed a buttered slice of bread on a plate, dropped an egg in its center and set it outside next to the coffee pot. By the time I had brushed my teeth, the coffee was ready, the toast crisp and the egg soft but not runny and ready to eat.

The dogs were slurping ice water at an alarming rate and although I refrigerated their kibble, it was steaming by the time I spooned it into their plates. The food was so hot, it gave Molly had heat blisters around her mouth. The poodle refused to take a chance and instead begged for human food each night after the blazing sun had finally set.

When the heat is as intense as it was that August, clothes become a handicap. I dressed in a pillowslip I had split at the top seam and elasticized around the top and protected my feet from the fiery pavement with tennis shoes. Nothing else. Every Wednesday, I put on my best Fieldcrest flowered pillow cover and the one pair of gym shoes I owned without holes at the bunion and walked to evening prayer meeting in the town center.

The church was nine miles from my trailer but I had to allow some time for stops along the way. I leashed the dogs and turned on all the fans in the place so the cat wouldn't become a roast before I returned and began my journey to communicate with the Lord. My first stop was three miles down the highway at a place called THE BLUE HOLE, a tree shaded quarry where all my buddies gathered to get high and stay cool. My friends Jonathan and Margie and their two children, Rachel and Jeremiah hung out there with their large Labrador mix, Brady, their owl, Who and their salamander, Gurgle. Margie hosed me off to cool me down and we all sipped sun tea before we continued our journey. We walked three miles further to Martha and Jud's farm. While the children climbed the gnarled fruit trees or swung in the tire hanging from the big oak out front, Martha hosed all five of us down. The sun dried us so quickly we had barely finished our tea before we were burned bright red. We finished our huge slices of bread baked on the kitchen windowsill and set out for town.

We stopped off at the post office to pick up Mrs. Redd, her daughter Shauna and their spaniel, Stamp. Mrs. Redd invited us in for iced tea while she filled up the mailbags for pick-up and then we continued to the Health Food Store, GOOD GRAINS FOR BETTER LIVING to remind everyone there that it was church night. Louise, Adam, their parrot Larynx and their trained muskrat, Bill closed the shop and joined our procession to the church.

By this time, there were 9 adults, 4 children 4 dogs, and a variety of wild life in our party. We arrived at the ramshackle building at the east end of town where everyone who hadn't been hospitalized for heat prostration was waiting with open arms. "Hey y'all," they chorused. "How do you like this here HEAT?"

We hugged each other and reminisced about last January's refreshing winter storm while we devoured our pot luck banquet of corn on the cob, tomato pudding, beans, fried okra, candied yams, zucchini bread, watermelon and more sun tea, all cooked to gourmet perfection on the front lawn. Then, we gathered in the main hall to give our thanks to the Lord. We thanked Him for food, shelter and for each other. We blessed Him for saving us from heat stroke and giving us each other. We all joined hands and filled the hall with a vigorous rendition of AMAZING GRACE because His grace was indeed wonderful to us.

That sizzling summer in Texas when the sun was so hot it cooked our dinner and the community spirit so strong if made us all feel treasured was indeed a beautiful experience for us all. We each became a brilliant jewel in a community necklace of love seasoned with our faith in the ultimate goodness of life. Whenever I begin to doubt the value of my existence or wonder if there is reason for hope in such a negative world, I remember those wonderfully loving people and I know that the human spirit is an everflowing fountain of goodness ready to give the least of us strength to ascend to our own special paradise.

Never be too wise recognize happiness
- Lynn Ruth

I Remember Jessica

We could never have loved the earth so well
If we had had no childhood in it.
- George Eliot

When I think of the happiness in my childhood, I remember Jessica. When I recall laughter and friendship, I see the two of us together in Birkhead Place. We lived four doors from one another and we were two parts of one person floundering in a world filled with mysterious rules we couldn't understand. Jessica was my first cousin and her mother was my Aunt Tick, the adult who did most to keep my ego from shattering under my mother's verbal hammer.

I see us now, standing on the brick road outside our homes. I am thin and dark with scabbed knees and circles under my eyes, wearing a smudged pair of jeans and my father's shirt. Jessica is four years younger than I and made of sturdier stock. Her frizzed blond hair frames cheeks pinked with outdoor play and incredibly blue eyes. Her jeans were muddied from rescuing grasshoppers, her nails blackened with digging for hidden treasures. She was a child who adored all living things not human. I can still picture her running from her home after a rainstorm to gather up the earthworms floating in the puddles that dotted our sidewalk. She draped them over the handlebars of her bicycle called, "I'm taking them for a ride to get dry! Meet me back at my house."

Her house was my refuge. It was a peaceful and clean place where my Aunt Tick never failed to welcome me with unmistakable delight. She was a woman who took me seriously in a world where my questions were called ridiculous and my fears labeled foolish. I adored her.

I entered that magic house where Tweety the canary twittered in the front hall and, in the kitchen, sick goldfish floated in water glasses. Hamsters ran on wheels in the bathroom and birdfeeders hung from every tree. There was always a dog underfoot. The first was Pee-Wee a long, long, long Dachshund, then Eric a smaller wiener dog followed by Dell an immense drooling boxer so exuberant he took whomever was on the other end of his leash on a flying airplane ride.

I remember our musical productions in my backyard where we made crepe paper costumes and sang popular songs, the lemonade we sold for a penny a glass and the bicycle rides over the bumps in the road. Our growing pains didn't hurt when we were together because we bandaged them with laughter. We giggled at private jokes, and at the people who didn't understand us. We saved our quarters and haunted candy stores that had fudge and mint Bavarian Crèmes. We shared them and hid the wrappers from our mothers so they wouldn't guess why we weren't hungry for dinner. We bought cracker jacks and traded our prizes and played jacks and Mother-May-I on the sidewalk.

In our turbulent teenage years, we found our only solace together. In the evening, Jessica would return to her room and I to mine to escape into our books and forget a world where we were supposed to wear lipstick and three inch heels. We pretended that we could dance as well as everyone else and Prince Charming was really what we wanted life to give us.

Jessica was an exceptional child, so intelligent that her parents sent her to an exclusive private school and that was the beginning of our drifting apart. Her world was that of the intellectual and mine was fighting for air in an inner city school. Still, we both attended fine universities, but I in my thirst to know everything there was to know, continued on to graduate schools. I dipped into two disastrous marriages. Jessica was a bridesmaid for the first one and I know she understood how frightened I was to take a step I knew was a false one.

I introduced her to the man who became her husband when I worked at our local television station and she married and left Toledo. I don't remember Jessica during those difficult years that followed. We were not letter writers and our talk never said what we communicated to one another.

More years passed and I became so sick I was hospitalized in a national hospital in the town that Jessica lived with her children. Once again, we were together and I saw the life she had fashioned. She was as devoted to her children as she had been to the goldfish and hamsters and dachshunds she mothered as a child. She gave up her every ambition to pour a fountain of enrichment and love into these two children and she succeeded. She was as rare a mother as she was a friend. She carried love to another dimension so strong it never wavered.

That is the Jessica I remember: the Jessica of laughter and song, crazy adventures and ridiculous escapades; the Jessica who cried "Lynnie, come help! Two dogs are stuck together in the middle of the street!"

I still see the Jessica that twirled a red white and blue baton while I sang "You're a Grand Old Flag"; the Jessica that climbed the cherry tree in our back yard or helped me shop for fashionable shoes that hurt my feet. That's the Jessica I knew.

Another Jessica, much older and incapacitated by cortical degeneration that paralyzed her for three years, died a week ago today. Another Jessica who had to be wheeled to concerts in a chair and write down her thoughts because there was a tube in her throat to send oxygen into her lungs. Her daughter wrote, " Mom was joyous to be around. We could make her laugh till the end. She was a fine person for being so sick. It hurts me so that I can't see her laugh again."

Thank God, that isn't the Jessica I recall. I am consoled always by the picture of a short happy little girl giving earthworms a ride in the sunshine, a beautiful human being who was the all of my childhood.

I often wonder what immortality is and I think it must be the sweetest memories we saved of the ones who loved us most. It must be the image we retain of those who gave us life saving gifts: acceptance and love. When I remember the only glory in my life, I remember Jessica. I think she would want it that way.

Count no hours but unclouded ones.
Let all others slip out of memory
- Harriet Beecher Stowe

Important Things

The future depends entirely on
What each of us does every day.
- Gloria Steinem

I was talking on the telephone when it happened. Can you imagine? I was gossiping with Sharon Grimes about Sally's lawn party when Jason's scream silenced me.

"Mama! Mama! Come quick!"

I dropped the telephone and ran outside. I felt like I had stumbled into a horror movie. There was my six-year-old son Jason trying to drag the baby out of the swimming pool.

I jumped into the pool, clothes and all and grabbed for them both. The water pulled at my skirt and it felt like a steel cord winding around my legs. I grabbed Benny and managed to bring him to the surface. I got out of the water with Jason paddling right behind me. I stood up and the dripping water mingled with my tears. My baby was dead. His body was limp; his skin was blue. I ran to the telephone and shouted, "Help someone! Get a doctor! Call an ambulance!"

I thought I was shouting at an operator. It was only later that I realized that I hadn't hung up the phone and Sharon was still on the line. It was she who dialed 911 and contacted the emergency rescue crew. She had to run next door to do it.

I was too frantic to think of things like that. I forgot the casserole baking in the oven. I forgot Joey. I forgot that I was dripping wet in a soaked skirt and blouse. All I knew was that my baby had stopped breathing and I had to save him.

I turned him upside down. Don't ask me why I did it. Maybe it was instinct. Maybe it was some fragment I had learned years ago in a forgotten lifesaving course. I think I figured some of the water that was choking him would run out of his mouth. I shook him and still he didn't move. "Hang on, Benny," I said. "Don't give up, honey. Try to breathe. Try!"

And I ran next door for help. I banged on the door but no one answered. I looked at Ben once more and my heart thundered against my ribs. My baby wasn't breathing. His tiny chest was still.

I had to get air into his lungs. Now. This minute. I laid him on the neighbor's step and breathed into his mouth. Nothing. I pried his mouth open and realized his tongue was folded backwards. It was keeping the air from getting past his throat. I dislodged it and tried forcing my breath into him once more. This time, he threw up. I kept breathing into my baby's mouth and willing him to live until I heard the sirens and knew help was on the way.

The rest was a bizarre nightmare. My whole world turned upside down. The ambulance attendant gave Benny oxygen while I held him in my arms. The sirens screamed and the wheels screeched as we roared through the city streets to the hospital. I tried not to think about my Jason all alone at home or my house with all the doors and windows wide open in the July heat.

Yes, Benny was saved. But it was only luck that rescued him. During those three days I sat with my son in the intensive care ward, I had lots of time to think. I still don't know what prompted me to turn the baby upside down or to breathe into his mouth the way I did. I had never seen mouth-to-mouth resuscitation done before, yet I knew instinctively that the only way to give Ben oxygen was for me to force it into him.

It still makes me shiver to think of all the things that could have gone wrong. What if the baby had inhaled so much water that it filled his lungs? What if he had gotten pneumonia? And what if I hadn't taught Jason to swim? Because it was Jason who really saved his brother. It was Jason who got my attention. It was he who dived in the pool to get Ben out. He managed to keep the baby's head above water. I took over where he left off.

In those three days that I sat at Ben's side and watched the color return to his face, I vowed to make a lot of changes in all our lives. I came too close to losing my baby because I got involved in a lot of gossip on the telephone. In a funny way, I'm glad the whole thing happened. We all get so caught up in our own affairs that we forget what's really important in life. I mean there I was rehashing a party and giggling on the telephone while my baby was drowning in the backyard pool. Benny's tragedy taught me what really matters in life. My family is my treasure. All the rest is trimming.

It's a lesson I'll never forget.

Tremble. Your whole life is a rehearsal
For the moment you are in now.
- Judith Malina

Keepsakes

Time flies over us, but leaves its shadow behind.
- Hawthorne

My mother and I battled each other every day we lived together and in every fight, my mother was the winner. She never stopped reminding me of the burden I was to her from the day I was born and the guilt I bore was almost too much to bear. I was convinced that my mother knew nothing and cared less about my frustrated dreams or the wrenching ache in my heart.

Now that I am older, I realize that she did indeed realize my pain. She showed it each time she bought me a gift.

I have always loved music. . .all kinds of music. In its wordless rhythms, I found solace for tears always ready to spill from my eyes. I will never forget the Christmas I came downstairs and there at the fireplace, was a portable phonograph that I could take to my room to play all the records I bought with every penny of my allowance. There, I could pretend I was the paper dolly someone loved and lost. I could believe I was the Juliet, Romeo died for.

My mother, whose words whipped me into submission, whose very glance reminded me of how useless I was, that woman I thought so cruel and unfeeling, realized that every little girl needs something that sweeps her out of herself into a lovely melody. She knew.

That year, I gave her a small stuffed bear I had made in Home Economics. It was white felt and I had stitched it with red thread in painstaking, even stitches. I sewed in tiny brown eyes and the smile I never dared to offer my angry mother. She opened this gift that had taken me hours and hours to create and pushed it aside. I was crushed and even the joy of having my own source of music, was soured by the way she disposed of the gift I had labored so long to create.

The next year was even harder for both of us. I hated coming home after school and I despised being me, because she had convinced me that I was worthless. That year I was pretty sure I would get nothing at all because I hadn't hidden my fury at the prison she had made for me. She was my enemy and I told her so every time she refused to let me sleep at my friend's house or go to a party. I screamed at her as shrilly as she did at me when she made me come home early from a party or insisted that I didn't deserve a new dress.

That holiday, I trudged downstairs with a gift I had made, in spite of myself. Deep in my heart, I could not believe that in reality my mother did not care for me. I recognized that somewhere far beneath the surface, I was bonded to my mother although that tie was protected by the armor I needed to survive her attacks. I handed her a black pincushion with a lace edge to it. I had not spent the time I spent on the little bear. Why bother? She wouldn't notice anyway.

She thrust my gift aside and pointed to the present she had for me. I barely hid my disappointment. I was sixteen years old and my mother gave me a life-sized doll. I was too old for such foolish playthings and I was devastated. I dragged the doll upstairs and when I put her on my bed, she looked so real, I felt she could actually speak to me. I realized then why my mother had given me so juvenile a gift. I had very few friends because she would not allow me to invite anyone over to our house after school. She and I never had a conversation. We only fought. My father ignored me and my sister took great pleasure in baiting me against my mother. There was no one to listen to the immense inner turmoil that almost choked me; no one to care that I dreamed of becoming a great writer; no one I could tell about my loneliness, my aching need to become a valuable person.

My mother sensed my desperate need and she filled it. She gave me a doll that would listen. I named it Penny and I ran up to my room after every quarrel, every success and every failure and I told that doll my secrets. I look back on my high school years and I am convinced that it was the release I felt after confiding in my silent little friend that kept me from turning to liquor or drugs to ease the terrible pain of those teen age years.

My mother and I gradually came to tolerate one another. It was only after she died that I realized how very many other gifts she had given this child she could not love. It was because of my mother that I got my college education. My father believed educating girls was a waste of time. My mother stood by me through my divorce because she knew how killing it is to live in a relationship that doesn't work. It was my mother who insisted my father help me get the house I live in now.

Once I was an adult, I accepted that I had no affection for the woman who bore me. I was certain that she didn't consider my moving to the other side of the country a loss to her. For me, that move to California began my life.

When she died, my sister sent me a box of the things my mother had kept as mementoes of my part in her life. I rifled though little cards I sent to my father and pictures of me as a child. As I fingered the fragments of my mother's treasures, I paused. There, wrapped in tissue so it wouldn't soil, was the tiny felt bear I had made for her, the small token of a love I wanted so much to feel. Right under it, was the black little cushion I made my sixteenth year.

My mother seemed hard as steel to me, but she was very human after all. Yet, no one bought her a phonograph so she could escape into music she loved even more than I. No one gave her a doll to listen and accept the troubles she buried deep inside her. She recognized my need because it was hers. She tried to make up for what she couldn't give me in the gifts she bought for me. I will never forget that doll or the tremendous joy I felt when I played my phonograph. I took those gifts with me wherever I went and always they consoled me. I never suspected that my mother treasured my gifts to her as much as I did those she had given to me. I like to think that perhaps they were her consolation.

Things that were hard to bear
are sweet to remember
- Seneca

A Love to Remember

How do I love thee?
Let me count the ways.
- Robert Browning

In 1958, I was hired to teach first grade at the Pierce Primary School in the slums of Brookline, Massachusetts. The children in my class had little to eat and less to wear. I think my dedication to those hungry, ragged urchins was magnified by shame that my own childhood had been so comfortable. I always had enough to eat and could choose anything I wanted from a filled closet to wear to school. My little Brookline children wore the same clothes each week until, by Friday, they were too soiled to distinguish their colors. The only hot meal they had was the breakfast the school fed them. When I was a child, I had teddy bears and Shirley Temple dolls. I rode a red three-wheeler with lots of chrome and had a yoyo that glowed in the dark. My pupils' toys were skipping ropes made from frayed clotheslines and lopsided balls they found in the gutter.

The child most deeply embedded in my memory from that year was Kevin O'Riley. "That kid is an incipient killer," warned Nancy Ward, the woman who taught him the year before. "The whole family is no good. I had the older brothers, too and they were so stupid, it was a miracle they found their way to school. This is Kevin's third year in first grade and frankly I doubt that he will ever see second grade."

To my amazement, the Kevin I met was the sweetest child in my room. He was affectionate and kind and always ready to help his classmates when they were in trouble. Although his social skills were superb, he had a terrible time with his schoolwork and part of the reason for this was that he was always a half hour late for school. When I asked him why he couldn't get there on time, he said, "I have to run to the doughnut shop to buy my mother her breakfast before I come to school. By the time I get back, the line for the bathroom is so long, I can't get in there in time.

Obviously, the reason Kevin was failing first grade was that his mother burdened him with so many unnecessary chores. I decided that a talk with his mother might remedy the situation. "Would you like me to go home with you today to meet your mom, Kevin?" I asked. "Maybe I can make her understand how important it is for you to get here on time."

He smiled. "Mama would love to meet you," he said. "She gets really lonesome because she has to stay home all day."

"Doesn't she go to work?" I asked.

Kevin shook his head. "She can't work because Daddy broke her arm the last time he was home," he said. "He hit her really bad and she has an awful bump on her head. She stumbles a lot and I have to carry the heavy things."

At three-fifteen, I dismissed my class and Kevin and I hurried down the junk littered street to his tenement building. He took my hand. "Be careful when you walk on the steps," he said. "We don't have any light in the hall anymore."

Together we climbed nine flights of stairs and Kevin led me past a community bathroom with the door ajar. One look convinced me that no one with a shred of personal hygiene would enter that disgusting cubicle. I swallowed my nausea and followed him to the end of the hall. He pushed open the door and called, "Wait 'til you see who came to visit you, Mama!"

He pulled me into a large room filled with children and empty bottles of liquor. A woman sat at a littered table with her head in her arms. At the sound of Kevin's voice, she lifted her head. "Kevin! Take this dollar and give it to Mr. Flaherty," she said. "Tell him mother needs her medicine. . . and hurry."

Kevin looked up at me and whispered, "She thinks I don't know what her medicine is but I do because Billy Winter's daddy drinks the same stuff. Mrs. Winter says all that alcohol will eat up Mr. Winter's liver."

Kevin gripped my hand and I could read the fear in his eyes. "I don't want my mother's liver to die," he said. "Because she might die with it."

Kevin went over to his mother and put his arms around her. "Mama," he said. "I've brought home that nice teacher I told you about!"

Mrs. O'Riley lifted her head and looked at me and then went back to sleep. Kevin's eyes filled. "I guess she needs to sleep it off," he said." When my mother isn't hurting so much, she's very nice, but now, her arm is so bent that she cries all the time."

I took his hand. "Come with me," I said. "I'll treat you to some groceries and then I have to hurry home."

This was a soap opera that I never believed could really happen and I was determined to help better this child's life if I possibly could. The next day, I went down to the principal and told him Kevin's story. The principal looked at me as if I were an innocent child. "Kevin's home life is no better or worse than any other child's in your class, Lynn Ruth," he said. "I'll tell the social worker to go over there but it won't do any good. We can clean up Mrs. O'Riley, but as soon as that no good husband of hers comes back, she'll get smashed up again and probably pregnant. Did you know that Kevin has twelve brothers and sisters, already?"

The next day, I packed a little lunch for Kevin to eat in the classroom and I did so for him every day after that. He and I became good friends and although I knew that his home was no refuge for him, I consoled myself that he and I had found a bit of sweetness together. That Valentine's s day, Kevin came to school with a terrible bruise on his cheek. His eye was black and the tears had not dried on his face." My mom did it," he said to my unspoken question. "I couldn't find any money for her doughnut."

He reached in his pocket and forced himself to smile. "Happy Valentine's Day, teacher!" he said and he handed me a flat package wrapped in red tissue with a white ribbon around it. I opened up the package realized why Kevin's mother had to sacrifice her coffee that morning. Her son spent the dollar on a white handkerchief with one tiny rose embroidered on the corner. The card with it said, "Be my valentine. Kevin."

I still have that hankie and each time I pull it out of my bureau drawer, I see Kevin's earnest face and that laboriously printed note. It reminds me that love comes in many packages and often involves cruel sacrifice. I don't know what happened to Kevin after I left, but I do know that any human being with his capacity to love at any cost cannot help but be a treasure to us all.

I love thee to the depth and breadth
and height my soul can reach
. . . I love thee with the breath,
smiles, and tears of all my life!
- Robert Browning

Loyalty

No act of kindness, no matter how small, is ever wasted.
- Aesop

When I was sixteen years old, Bradley Cramer nominated me for Queen of the Snowballs. I ran against Dorothy Shapiro whose daddy made gorgeous false teeth and even prettier daughters. The third contender was the rabbi's daughter, Paula Goldberg.

Bradley Cramer was one of my favorite friends but I think I was his only one. His mama supported him by working for her brother in his fish market because she didn't have a husband. Every day, Sadie Cramer got up before dawn to clean her house and get Bradley dressed for school and pack his lunch before she hurried off to sell fish at her brother's market until six at night. When she packed Bradley his very substantial meal, she made at least four cold fish sandwiches, two different kinds of home made cookies and little treats like a penny for the gum ball machine or a pop up toy to make him laugh. By noon, you could smell Bradley the minute he walked into the cafeteria because those fish sandwiches had gotten very warm and aromatic in the cloakroom. The minute he walked through the door, all the school kids would giggle and whisper "Fish!"

When he sat down at a table, everyone picked up their lunches and moved away. His face would turn very red and his smile would fade into a terrible sadness that broke my heart. If I saw him in time, I always waved at him and called, "Cub sit here with be, Bradley! There's pleddy of roob!"

That lunch box was really very pungent, but I could stand anything if I could just make him not notice how cruel everyone was to him.

Bradley had a terrible time in school and I think it was because everyone made such fun of him that he couldn't concentrate. When I saw him in study hall laboriously trying to write down words he couldn't spell about things like the Russian Revolution or the crops they grew in Bombay, I could feel tears gather in my eyes. I sat next to him as often as I could and I helped him with his homework. I didn't want to embarrass him, so I just peered at his open book and pointed to the answer to the questions.

I thought it was very unfair that he should suffer just because he didn't know who his father was and his mother had to sell fish for a living.

Everyone else had brothers and sisters who protected them and helped them through the painful storm of growing up. Sadie Cramer was too busy to stand up for Bradley and probably too tired. If one of the kids who made fun of Bradley flunked history, that person's mother could afford private tutors to help him, but Sadie Cramer was a grade school drop out who never got past the sixth grade.

If one of Bradley's tormentors didn't like the way his lunch smelled, he could throw it out and buy something else to eat. But Bradley Cramer always dressed in his cousin Ronnie's cast off clothes with the legs too short and the jackets too tight because he had no extra money to spend. His mama couldn't afford to buy him his own shirts much less give him an allowance. Instead she gave him more important things like the kind of love that never wavers and time to be with him when he needed her most. Instead of taking a lunch hour, she left the fish market at three o'clock to pick up her little boy from school and bring him back to the market. He did his homework while Sadie served her brother's customers. At night, Sadie brought her love child home, cooked him a hot meal and after an hour or so together watching television, or playing Chinese checkers, she put them both to bed.

When we were in high school, Bradley always came to the mixers at the Jewish Community Center or the dances at the high school, alone. No one would go out with him because he didn't have a car and couldn't afford fancy treats or corsages. When he walked into the room, all dressed up in Ronnie's frayed white shirt and a garish tie Sadie found on sale at Woolworth's, everyone would laugh and whisper "Fish!"

As soon as I smelled him, I excused myself and ran over to say hello, because he looked so desolate and all alone. Bradley loved to dance and so did I, so as soon as he saw me, his face brightened and he said, "Hey, Lynnie! How about a dance?"

Well, I want to tell you, that boy had magic in his feet! I just loved to fly around the floor in his arms. The big band music moved very fast and the beat was loud as thunder. My toes skimmed the floor when we sailed through "The Muskrat Ramble" and "Sing, Sing, Sing." and my eyes flashed like blazing stars.

I had lots of dates during those four years. Some were handsome, some clever and there were even a few who thought they adored me. But I never had as much fun with any of them as I did with Bradley Cramer when our shoes sparked like flint on stone as we whirled across that waxed floor at the Jewish Community Center gym.

Every January, we had a big competition at the Center for Queen of the Snowballs. In our junior year, Bradley told me he had nominated me and I was shocked. I knew very well that I was no beauty queen. I told a good joke, but I didn't make a very pretty picture. My competition was far superior to me. Paula was a gracious, lovely person with the support of the entire Conservative Jewish community. Dorothy Shapiro was movie star pretty. She was the most popular girl in the Junior class. With that kind of competition, I knew I didn't stand a chance.

Snow Ball Queen nominees were supposed to invite their escorts instead of the other way around because he would be King of those Snowballs, if she won. I asked Paul Benjamin, a very handsome pharmacy student at Toledo University because drove a yellow convertible and could afford a decent corsage.

The dance was held in The Secor Hotel Ballroom and I wore a purple strapless gown I rounded out with bath powder mitts so it wouldn't fall down. When I saw Bradley walk into the room, I excused myself as I always did and hurried over to say hello. He flushed with pleasure and held out his arms. "May I?" he asked.

"Of course!" I said.

The band was super hot that night and the two of us really moved. The dance style then was to face your date, hold both his hands and move out and then back together to the beat. Every time our bodies slammed together as we galloped across the floor, little clouds of bath powder puffed up from my bodice and Bradley would smile and say, "Gee, Lynnie! You smell really GOOD!"

The band played "String of Pearls" and then swung into "A Shanty in Old Shanty Town" and Bradley sent me flying through the air in a flurry of tulle and bath powder. I was in heaven.

When the set was over, Bradley returned me to Paul Benjamin who was trying to come on to Dorothy Shapiro's sister, Rose Anne. "May I dance with you when you're the Queen?" asked Bradley and I blushed as purple as my dress.

Paul Benjamin was talking to Rose Anne Shapiro and didn't notice I had returned. Bradley tapped him on the shoulder. "You won't mind, will you?" he asked.

"Mind what?" asked Paul.

At midnight, everyone gathered at the bandstand and the president of B'nai B'rith announced the winner. Dorothy Shapiro smoothed her make up and fluffed her pageboy bob. The rabbi's daughter looked down at her hands in a suitably modest manner and I tried to look like A Noble Loser.

"Our Queen," said Mr. Feldstein. "Is little Lynnie Miller!"

I could not believe what I'd heard. My face flushed and suddenly I felt very beautiful and very proud that I had beaten out the rabbi's daughter and glamorous Dorothy Shapiro even though I was flat-chested and wore braces. When all the clapping and the shouting died down, Bradley Cramer came up to me said. "Let's show them how to dance, Lynnie." and took me in his arms.

We left poor Paul Benjamin doing the best he could with Gloria Axelrod and we cut a spectacular rug. The powder puffed like mushroom clouds and we sailed across the floor in a perfumed aura of purple tulle and pounding feet. At the end of the dance I gasped, "Thank you so much Bradley. Dancing with you was even better than winning that contest."

He blushed very red and he said. "I knew you'd win, Lynnie."

"How on earth could you know a thing like that?" I asked.

He grinned. "I knew because I voted for you 538 times."

When I recall that night, I always feel terribly sad. The only one who learned something of real value was Dorothy Shapiro. She realized she could never trade on her beauty in life and that is a very good thing. The rabbi's daughter thought she wasn't popular enough for anyone to vote for her. And I? I still weep when I realize that Bradley Cramer was so grateful to me for no reason that I could see. All I had done was treat him with the common human decency every human being deserves.

An ounce of loyalty is worth a pound of cleverness
- Elbert Hubbard

The Missing Ring

Persecution for opinion is
The master vice of society
Francis Wright

Nancy Morgan hurried into the house and put her bag of groceries on the kitchen counter. "Hi, Dolly," she said to the gray cat rubbing itself against her legs. "What have you been up to since I left? Eating all the breakfast leftovers?"

She looked at the pile of greasy breakfast dishes piled in the sink and sighed. She glanced at the kitchen clock. "Two o'clock already?" she said. "I better get busy. Jeremy will be home from school pretty soon and I haven't even begun to clean up this mess."

She hung up her coat, put on her apron and started to work. First, she put away the groceries. Then, she took off her jewelry and put it on the kitchen windowsill. She rolled up her sleeves and began to do the dishes. Just as she was scouring the last pan, the telephone rang.

She wiped her hands on her apron and ran for the phone. "Hello?" she said, breathlessly. "Martha? No, nothing's wrong. I was in the kitchen and I had to hurry into the den to catch your call. I hoped it was you. We'd better firm up our plans for the church rummage sale. It begins next week and we haven't even begun to find our workers. Just a minute. I'll get a pencil and paper."

Nancy settled herself in a comfortable chair with a pad of paper on her lap. This was going to be a long conversation.

As she and Martha became involved in their plans, she heard the kitchen door open. "Just a second, Martha," she said. "Jeremy is that you?"

"Yes, Mom. Is there anything I have to do before I can go outside? Randy and I want to ride our bikes for a while."

"No, honey. There's milk in the refrigerator if you want it or an apple."

"Great! Can Randy have some milk, too? Any cookies?"

"In the breadbox. And be sure to wash your glasses. I don't want to find a mess when I get off the phone."

"Sure, Mom. I promise."

"Sorry, Martha. Now, what were you saying? Oh yes. I agree with you. I don't think we'd better ask Susan Garfield, either. She's had her hands full with Randy these days. I doubt if she'll have any extra time. Besides, she has to take him for therapy every weekend. My God! That was Randy Jeremy had with him just now; and I left my jewelry on the window sill! Listen, Martha, wait one more second. I want to check to make sure it's all there. I'm especially worried about my diamond ring. It's an heirloom from Bob's mother. . . . just the kind of thing Jeremy would take. If I don't catch him right away, he'll have it hidden where no one can find it."

She put down the telephone and hurried into the kitchen. Sure enough, the ring was missing. Her watch and her bracelet were still on the sill. "Funny," she thought. "Why did he leave those? Why didn't he just take all of it?"

She shrugged her shoulders and returned to the telephone. "Look, Martha. I'll have to call you back. My ring is missing and I want to see if I can catch Randy before he gets home. I would hate to have to bother Susan with this."

She hung up the telephone and went outside. She saw her son playing ball with several other boys but Randy Garfield wasn't one of them. "Jeremy!" she called. "Jeremy! Can you come here a minute?"

"What's wrong, Mom?" asked Jeremy as he approached her. “You look upset? Didn't I clean up the kitchen right?"

"No, no, honey it's not that. Jeremy, where is Randy?"

"He had to go home. He had an appointment with the school counselor this afternoon."

"Oh, I see. Listen, Jeremy, when you were in the kitchen, did you see my jewelry?"

"Your jewelry? Oh, yeah! It was on the windowsill. There was a bracelet and a watch."

"That's right, a bracelet and a watch. Did you see anything else?"

"Gosh, I don't remember, Mom. I really didn't pay much attention."

"Jeremy, my ring was there too. You know. The ring grandma gave me last year. Didn't you see that, too?"

Jeremy thought for a moment. " I don't remember seeing it, but I'm not sure. Why? Oh, I get it! You think Randy took it! Well, he didn't, Mother. I know he didn't. I was with him every single minute he was in the kitchen. Besides, he's really over that, now. He hasn't stolen anything for at least three months. He was explaining to me about it. He has a disease called kleptomania and since he's been going to the doctors, he's almost cured."

"I'm sure he has improved a great deal, Jeremy; but my ring is missing and he was the only one who could have taken it. You didn't leave him to go to the bathroom or anything, did you?"

"No, I didn't. I'll bet it just fell on the floor or something. Did you look?"

"No," said Nancy. "I just noticed it was missing about five minutes ago and I wanted to catch Randy before he disposed of it."

"That's not fair, Mom. You didn't even try to find it first."

"I guess you're right, honey. Come on. Let's go in and look for it together."

The two of them entered the house and began to search the kitchen. They looked on the counter and Jeremy crawled around the floor but they found nothing.

"Do you think it fell down the drain?" asked Jeremy.

"No, it couldn't have. I had the lid on the disposal and the other sink was filled with soapy water. I was scouring the frying pan when the telephone rang. We just now emptied the sink with the strainer in the drain and nothing turned up. I'm sorry, honey, but it had to be Randy Garfield. Diamond rings don't disappear into thin air. I'll tell you what. Before I report this to the insurance company, I'll call Susan. If she can get him to return it, then I won't say anything and Randy won't have another black mark on his record. Okay?"

"Okay, Mom," said Jeremy slowly. "But all you're going to do is upset everyone there because I'm positive Randy didn't take your ring."

"Well, I hope you're right," said Nancy. "But I want to call Susan, anyway. Otherwise, I'll have to report it to the insurance company. The Garfields will be a lot more upset when the company begins its investigation. They'll have to notify the school and the juvenile court, and then Randy will be in real trouble."

Nancy left her son still looking for her ring and went into the library. She picked up the telephone. "Hello, Susan?" she said. "Do you have a minute? I had a rather disturbing thing happen this afternoon. I had my diamond ring on the windowsill and had to leave to answer the telephone. While I was talking, Randy and Jeremy came into the kitchen and now the ring is missing. I really hate to bother you with this, but Jeremy and I have torn the kitchen apart trying to find it and it just isn't there. I wonder if you could ask Randy about it. He was the only one in the kitchen who could have taken it and I'm afraid he might have had a relapse or something."

Susan Garfield was distraught. "Oh, Nancy, we've worked so hard to keep him from doing that again. The juvenile authorities said that if he took one more thing, he'd have to be put in a detention home where he can get counseling and psychotherapy daily. I would just hate to do that to Randy. He's such a sweet kid. Kleptomania is a disease, you know. It's not as if my son were a thief. Have you told anyone about it yet?"

"No," answered Nancy. "I know how awful this would be for you if he did take it. I decided to call you and let you talk to him. If you can get him to return the ring, I'll just forget it happened. Okay?"

"Oh, Nancy! You're a gem! I'll talk to him right now and if he knows anything at all, I'll let you know."

"If you can't find out anything, Susan, I'll have to report this to the insurance company first thing in the morning. I'm sorry, but it's a valuable ring and Bob would be just sick if we lost it. It's been in his family for years."

"I understand," said Susan. "I'll call as soon as I'm done talking to Randy. If he has it, I'm sure we'll have it back to you tonight."

"I hope so, Susan. I would hate to be the one responsible for sending Randy into a detention home."

Nancy was just cleaning up the dinner dishes when Susan called.

"I just finished talking to Randy," she said. "And Nancy, he swears he knows nothing about your ring. He says he saw a bracelet and a watch on the windowsill and was really proud of himself because he wasn't even tempted to take them. But he didn't see a ring. I know my son and I don't think he's lying, Nancy."

Nancy sighed. "Well, I guess that settles it, doesn't it. I'll have to call the insurance company in the morning. Meanwhile, Jeremy and I will keep looking for the ring. It just might turn up somewhere; you never can tell."

The next morning, Nancy just couldn't bring herself to call the insurance company. "I'll do it later", she thought. "I just hate to cause all this trouble for the Garfields."

She went into the bathroom and began to empty the kitty litter. As she scooped through the sand she saw something glitter and then she smiled. She looked at the cat who was observing her as she worked. "Why, Dolly!" she laughed. "You certainly have expensive taste! Won't Susan be thrilled to hear what you ate yesterday!"

People are almost always better
Than their neighbours think they are.
- George Eliot

The Attack

Cruelty, like every other vice, requires
No motive outside itself
It only requires opportunity.
- George Eliot

It was a day like any other. She worked in her garden; she walked her dogs; she stopped at Charlotte's before she went to the store. "Do you want anything?" she asked.

The older woman shook her head. "No. I think I'm set for dinner tonight. Oh yes. If you see some lemons, I could use a few."

She smiled. "I'll see lemons. How many?"

Charlotte handed her a dollar. "One or two," she said. "You're not going out tonight are you?"

She pushed the dollar away. "My treat," she said. "Of course I'm going out. Why shouldn't I?"

The other woman shook her head. "Didn't you see the paper?" she asked.

The younger woman looked puzzled and then she nodded. "You mean that article about the young lady who was attacked in Side Cut Park?" she asked. "What does that have to do with me?"

"That's the third time he's struck this month, Louise," said Charlotte and she waved the banner headline like an SOS signal. "He always goes after women out alone after dark and you walk those dogs every night."

She smiled and patted Charlotte's arm. "And I'll walk them again tonight," she said. "You're sweet to worry, Charlotte, but don't. People ask for the trouble they get. Besides, he attacks girls. I'm hardly that, anymore."

Charlotte shook her head. "Every age looks good in the dark, honey. This guy is a maniac."

She shrugged. "If I let things like that bother me, I'd never go anywhere. I could get killed by a car, too. You have to take chances if you want to live, Charlotte. And I want to live. I love to live."

She smiled and started back to her car. "I'll bring you the lemons," she said.

The clock raced toward seven. She dressed and hurried to her concert. Brahms. His third symphony. She loved that one. It reminded her of college. They used to play it in the dorms all the time.

She was humming the first movement theme when she came home. It was ten o'clock. She had to walk the dogs one last time. She clipped their leashes to their collars and flipped the porch light on. "We're not afraid of bogey men are we, guys?" she asked.

They wagged their tails. She reached into her pocket and gave each a biscuit. "Mama's darlings," she said and she smiled. "Ready?"

Her beautiful day was winding down. She took a hot bath and got ready for bed. There wasn't much that was unusual about the past twenty-four hours. They formed a day like any other, filled with simple pleasures she thoroughly enjoyed. She closed her notebook and put it on the table. She picked up her book.

The dogs were flat out at her feet. She rubbed Molly's ears. Cindy stretched and moved to her lap. Jake rolled over and began to snore. She kissed Cindy's head and the dog snuggled against her. She put on her glasses and leaned back against her pillow. She was reading a mystery she couldn't put down. She adjusted the lamp and lost herself in the story. A young man was trying to outwit the FBI and the Mafia and it looked like he just might succeed. Her eyes devoured the pages.

She read for three hours and forced herself not to flip to the end. Her eyes burned. She reached for the light switch and paused. She decided she was hungry. She put on her robe and took her novel into the kitchen with her. She hadn't had time for a proper dinner. . . just a sandwich and coffee . . . and she was suddenly famished. The dogs pattered after her into the kitchen. She leaned down to pet them. "And biscuits for you!" she said. "I promise."

She pulled out a casserole of turkey from the refrigerator and put it in the oven. She filled the teakettle and stopped. She turned off the flame. She plugged in the coffee grinder on the counter and spooned out some coffee beans. "Why not?" she said. "I deserve a treat. No instant tonight. It's French roast or nothing!"

The tiny kitchen bubbled with the rich brown aroma of the casserole and perking coffee. The dogs sat on their haunches, paws up. She laughed and kissed their noses. "Your turn will come," she said. "Be patient!"

She heard footsteps outside and glanced at the clock.

Two a.m.

She was furious. "Another lousy bastard on the back porch! Why does he have to cross my lawn to go next door? What's wrong with the street?"

She could hear the clatter of his heels as he climbed over the fence. Well! This time she'd stop him. This time, she'd really give him hell! She yanked the back door open.

"You get out of there!"

He stood before her, a giant shadow in the doorway.

She froze.

She tried to push the door shut.

Too late.

He grabbed her by the collar and hit her face. Her head snapped to one side, then the other. She stared at his blurred image, horrified.

His features were stone.

Why are you doing this? she screamed.

Her voice gurgled in her throat and her words died. She heard the thud of her body as it fell to the floor, but she felt nothing.

I don't even know you. You are a horrible dream. Yes. That's it. Any minute I'll wake up and you'll be gone. You're that dill pickle I couldn't refuse. Do you understand? YOU ARE NOT REAL.

He struck her harder, again and then again. She crashed into the Tiffany lamp. It clattered to the floor in a blue shower of broken glass. He used her collar like a leash to lift her above the debris. His free hand smashed into her face.

Once more, she tried to scream but her voice froze. Her body was swollen with sensation: white, hot pain, impossible shock. "Stop! STOP!"

The words rumbled in her throat. Her eyes filled with blood. It poured down her face and soaked into her robe. She could taste it, sour and bitter. . . awful.

Oh God, please make him quit. Why are you letting him do this to me? He's going to kill me.

He dragged her across the floor. Her hips bounced against the hardwood boards. The jagged edges of the smashed light bulb ground into her legs. Her slipper caught in the heat vent. She could feel her ankle twist as the shoe wrenched from her foot.

Her eyes refused to focus. The room whirled around her like a movie reel escaping from its spool. The dining room table danced on marshmallow legs; the living room couch squashed into a misshapen ball.

Her robe twisted and her neckband tightened around her throat. She gasped for air. Her eyes bulged and her tongue filled her mouth like a saturated sponge. He pulled her into the bedroom.

"No! NO!"

At last, her voice worked. It sounded like a warped record, a wild, banshee moan. She could hear it accelerate into knives of sound that sliced the blood-thickened air.

He stopped.

He threw her limp body against the wall. She crumbled to the floor and skidded in a pool of her own blood.

He turned and wiped his hands on his pants. She stared, immobilized as the stain of her blood spread across his black corduroy hips. He tore open the bolted front door as if the locks were paper.

He was gone.

She stumbled to the telephone. Got to dial Operator. Got to get help.

She heard a cracked, frantic voice force itself out of her throat. "I've been attacked. I think I need help. I can't stop the bleeding. 2925 Glendale. Hurry. Oh, please hurry."

Did that loathsome sound come from her throat? Impossible. She dropped the receiver. She stared at red streaked walls and carmine pools splashed across the floor. "Must clean it up . . . now."

She staggered into the bathroom and wet a towel with cold water. Her blood dripped into the wet sink and spread like batik dye. She looked up into the mirror. Who was that?

A grotesque mask stared back at her. Its right eyebrow was pushed half way to its hairline. Its nose was bent almost flat. Its mouth was frozen into a tight, pursed knot. Blood dripped down its lacerated chin.

That couldn't be me!

She got down on her knees and wiped up her footprints even as fresh blood fell to the floor. She held another rag to her face and washed the telephone. She worked in a daze. She soaked the stained towels in cold water. She rubbed them with soap that burned into the abrasions in her hands. She scrubbed until the stains had disappeared down the drain. She plugged the sink and soaked the towels again. Then, she remembered dinner.

She forced herself to hurry into the kitchen. She turned off the oven.

Sirens.

"Thank God."

She weaved into the living room and clutched the couch for support. The room rolled around her like a crazy ferris wheel. The broken door was still ajar. She saw the two policemen enter through a veil of her own blood. She staggered across the floor into their arms. She could smell the freshness of outdoors on their rough wool coats. She clung to them and tried to speak.

It was no use. She'd lost all her words. All she could give them were tears. Wild, body wrenching sobs.

"All right, lady. Try to calm down. Tell us exactly what happened. What did he look like? Have you ever seen him before?"

She shook her head. "He was dressed all in black like a silhouette and he smelled like. . ."

She frowned, puzzled. Then she nodded. "He smelled like jasmine, that's it.. . . just like those bushes in Charlotte's front yard. He pushed his way through my back door and hit me."

She swallowed hard. Her eyes darted from one man to the other and she gripped their sleeves. "Why did he do that? I don't even know him. He dragged me into the bedroom and I thought . . . I thought . . . . "

She looked up at the men and her eyes overflowed. She paused and swallowed. "Then, he stopped."

She began to cry again.

"We're going to take you to the hospital. You need stitches or your face is going to look like a rat's maze."

She shook her head. "I want to go to bed. I'm so tired. . . so tired."

"Lady. Your face won't wait. You might get some kind of infection. Where is your coat? Here. Put it on."

She grabbed her purse and hesitated. She reached for her book. This might take a while and she was almost finished with the story. The two men helped her out the door. She heard the screeching sirens and felt the jolt of the squad car as it tore through stopped traffic. Then the world went blank.

The first nightmare was over.

The second was about to begin.

The hospital doors opened. She clung to the two policemen. The tiled floor undulated like a distorted ocean. Her legs were foam rubber, her eyes warped glass. She turned her head away from the light. "I'm so cold . . so cold," she said.

She tried to focus on the scrambled panorama before her. The place was electric with activity. Masked figures in white, bustling women with pink striped dresses, attendants pushing wheelchairs, interns waving charts, moving, always moving. The antiseptic smell choked her. She felt like she had been dumped into a fresh scrubbed latrine.

A wheelchair whizzed so close she curled her toes. A baby cried. A woman burst out of one of the curtained partitions. She held a cloth to her mouth and fell against the reception desk. A man carried a screaming child in his arms. The little boy kicked and pounded his fists on his father's chest. The child's shoe flew across the room. It bounced on the wheel of an empty gurney and landed on the floor.. . . a tiny red sneaker, bulging at the toe, run down at the heel. It lay on its side, empty and unnoticed.

She felt blood trickle down her forehead. She looked for the policemen. "I want to go home." she said.

But the two men had vanished. She was alone.

She watched the medical staff rush past her. She tried to grab a sleeve, an apron string, a glance. "Please, let me lie down."

No one heard her.

Her knees felt like melting jello. She reached for the wall. She touched the cold plaster and felt herself drift out of reality. And then, as if by magic, she was the center of activity. A face appeared, a hand took her arm. Efficient people, knowing women took charge. They propelled her into a screened in cubicle and drew the plastic curtains. A nurse removed her clothes. "Oh dear," she said. "I'm going to have to pull this off. It's stuck to your skin. You poor little thing."

Don't feel sorry for me or I'll start crying and I must not do that. I must not.

The woman tied her hospital gown. "All set, darling," she said. "Dr. Winter will fix you all up good as new."

The nurse stroked her hair and smoothed it away from her forehead.

More tears. God damn the tears. They made her feel helpless, weak. "I'm terribly cold," she whispered.

Blankets. Hot water bottle. Maternal sounds that made no sense.

"Doctor will be right in, love," said the nurse.

She was alone again.

She groped in her purse and found the book. She opened the pages and the print dissolved into rivulets of ink across the page. She closed her eyes. Her pulse thundered in her ears. Her head throbbed and her leg felt wet with blood. She hadn't even noticed her leg before.

"My goodness! You look awful. Sorry we couldn't get to you sooner. Had a baby in convulsions and a motorcycle crash just before you got here. Crazy isn't it? Quiet as the morgue all night and then at midnight all hell broke loose. Must be a full moon."

What? Oh, yes. This one was a doctor.

"I didn't see the moon."

Or the stars or the road or anything but flashing lights and the blood that filled my eyes.

He had a stethoscope around his neck. He was two darting irises and a green mask. She looked at the receding hair, the creases in that forehead and tried to reconstruct a face. It was no use. This was a uniform and some forceps. It brought no comfort. It could not heal.

His fingers probed her forehead and then pulled back the sheet. "Looks like you bumped into an enraged mixmaster."

She shut her eyes and saw HIS face, a stone mask, silent, cold, evil.

She shivered and shook her head. "Not quite," she said.

He smiled and she became a person once more. "Hold still," he said.

He poked at her face with gentle fingers, careful little touches that forced the life back into her. "I'll have to take stitches in this eyebrow . . . your leg, too. Your nose is pretty bad."

She smiled. "I can still smell," she said.

"That's not what I meant."

He paused and pushed at the bridge of her nose. "I think I can straighten it," he said.

"That hurt," she said.

"It's all over," he said. "You're pretty as a picture."

"That's a switch. I was a middle aged disaster before."

"My God! A comedian! I can't believe it!"

She couldn't believe it either. Why this sudden euphoria? What happened to the lassitude that smothered her only minutes before? Now, she felt full of fun . . fun, for God's sake. She was wide awake. She chattered, she quipped, she laughed and entertained.

She looked at the clock on the wall. Three thirty.

"You sure there isn't a full moon?" he asked.

"Positive."

She returned home at four in the morning, exhilarated still. She thanked the police who drove her from the hospital. She kept talking in a wild attempt to keep them with her. It didn't work. They left her at her front door and once again, she was alone.

Except for the dogs. They barked. They bounded to her and licked her feet, jumped for her face, rolled across the rug. "Why didn't you do this when HE was here?" she asked.

She sat down on the floor and let them love her. She took Cindy into her arms and buried her face in Molly's fur. "My babies. My wonderfuls. Mama's here. Mama's back. Oh my little loves!"

More tears. Would they never stop?

She stood up. "That hurt."

She pointed to the bedroom. The three dogs trotted over to the bed. She leaned against the door and felt a hundred years old. The place was chaos. Her heart walloped her ribs and her head felt like tissue paper. She forced herself to concentrate on one action at a time. She moved slowly, and methodically to set things right.

She propped a chair under the doorknobs of both doors and looked once more at the debris. She sighed. She picked up her purse from the floor. She hung her coat in the closet. She scraped the dried blood from the carpet, the walls and the telephone. She soaked the rags. She sat down and tried to center herself. "What was I doing before HE came?"

She looked around the tidy room. Her eyes rested on the table. It was set for a meal.

"That's it. I was heating turkey."

She got up from her chair and forced her legs to take her into the cramped pullman kitchen. It was still warm and smelled of food. The coffee pot was cold to the touch. She lit the flame. "I need you right now," she told the liquid.

She looked at the door. It had scuff marks and streaks of dirt and blood. She sprayed the evidence of her struggle with Windex and it was gone. She tested the knob. The door was locked. She leaned her forehead against the wood panels. She had wiped out the visible remains of the attack, but how could she erase this terror? Windex couldn't do that.

She pulled her casserole out of the oven. It smelled like comfort and she wanted it. "No use going to bed, now," she told the dogs. "I'm too wound up."

She pulled off bits of meat for Jake and cut up the liver for Cindy and Molly. "Dog biscuits for dessert," she promised.

Molly lapped at her ankle. She knelt beside the fuzzy puppy and buried her bandaged face in the silken fur. She felt the solidity of the dog's body and that was real. Jake licked her face and she could feel his sturdy ribs and steady heart beat. That, too was real. Only this night was a mirage.. . . an endless black fantasia. She clung to the puppy in her arms. "Oh, lovey," she said. "Oh my lovey."

She stood up and put on her apron. She worked in the kitchen by rote. Her routines soothed her. Her breathing slowed and her thoughts centered on her task. She set her book on the table and read as she ate. She washed the dishes and let out the dogs. She swept the floor and scoured the sink. She undressed and brushed her teeth. She opened the medicine cabinet door so she wouldn't have to see her face. She opened the back door. "Bed!" she called.

She propped the chair under the doorknob and secured the chain bolt. The three dogs hopped on the coverlet and she crawled under the blanket. She held them close and felt their needing her. She nuzzled her face into Jake's black fur. The dogs felt warm and forever to her. She closed her eyes.

It was six o'clock Sunday morning.

She slept until ten Monday night. She felt swollen, lumpy as a bag of potatoes. The dogs bolted for the door. "I hear you," she said.

She wrapped the blanket around her and took the chair away from the back door. The animals bounded into the yard. She went into the bathroom and looked in the mirror.

Who was that?

Two black eyes, a bandaged forehead and a broken nose. Black and blue smudges, yellow, red and purple marks, cuts, scabs. Where was the skin? Pain. Oh my Lord. How can one body ache like this? It isn't fair. It can't be true.

She touched her face. It was true, all right.

She stretched across the rumpled bed. "Just for a minute," she said. "So tired. So awfully tired."

She awoke Tuesday night. She had not seen daylight for over forty eight hours. She got out of bed. The dogs scratched on the back door.

"I'm coming," she called. "I'm COMING."

The second nightmare was over.

It was the third nightmare that wouldn't end.

She was combing her hair when the dogs barked. She locked the bathroom door and listened. She waited. She felt fear wash over her and she was limp. He's back. He's in the living room waiting for me.

She took a deep breath and turned the knob. The house was empty.

She put on her coat and hooked the leashes on the dogs. She stood at her front door, paralyzed.

What if he's on the porch?

She squared her shoulders and opened the door. Her eyes narrowed. You robbed me of forty eight hours of my life, you lousy bastard. I am not giving you one minute more.

She pulled in two newspapers from the front porch. She opened Monday's and scanned the headlines. There was no mention of her attack. She ruffled through the rest of the paper. Nothing. It hadn't even made the back page. She put the paper next to the couch and once more walked out the door.

She stepped outside, the three dogs pulling at her arm. She walked down the street and she saw him in every face. She shut her eyes and he was there. But when the police inspector came, she couldn't describe him. "He was tall, dark, and very clean. He smelled like flowers. I'm not sure I'd recognize him if I saw him but I'd know that smell. I never really looked at him because I was trying to shield my face. I didn't do a very good job, did I?"

She blushed and looked down at her hands. They were trembling and her voice was very near the breaking point. She swallowed. "He must live near here. I didn't hear a car pull away and my door was wide open. That's why I'm so afraid to go outside. I might run into him and God only knows what he'll do to me this time.

"Sure I know how lucky I am. I could have been raped. I could have been crippled. I could have been killed. But I wasn't and I don't feel lucky at all."

During the first week after the attack, she was besieged with curiosity seekers. They knocked on her door to see her wounds and offer unwanted advice, unrealistic and too late. "Did you recognize him?"

"No."

"Better put ice packs on that eye or it will swell."

"Yes."

"Why didn't you call me? I would have come right over and shot him. I keep my gun loaded all the time."

He was gone now and their words could not erase the scars he left behind. She would wear them on her face until the day she died.

Charlotte brought her soup and but she pushed the bowl away. "I'm not ready for that, yet," she said.

The other woman looked puzzled. "How can you not be ready for soup?" the woman asked.

She bit her lip. She cleared her throat to hide the quaver in her voice. "I'm just not," she said. "Thanks, anyway."

She shut the door and watched her only friend on the block trudge back home, hurt and puzzled by an attack she didn't understand. The rejected soup spattered from its bowl leaving a dark trail on the cement.

Her telephone would not stop ringing. She unplugged it so she could be alone to heal her wounds. She snapped and snarled at her well-meaning neighbors. They invaded her privacy at all hours with homemade treats, casseroles to reheat and coffee cake they hoped she'd invite them to share. She didn't. She rejected their gifts through a crack in the door and locked herself back into her apartment before they had a chance to force themselves inside.

In a few weeks, her pain eased and she began to feel her isolation. She needed people who didn't pry; friends who could take her mind out of herself. But now, no one came. She had driven them all away.

Her bitterness ballooned inside her. Her lovely days had vanished. She had no pleasures anymore. Where was that sweet little lady who trusted everyone and treasured her world? She was gone forever. This new woman was cold and hard. She had learned to hate. She nourished her seeds of malice with self-pity and bitterness.

He's out there living his life, not a scratch or a bruise on him.

She could almost see him: tall, vigorous, full of life, laughing with his cronies as he told them about that old maid he scared hell out of a few months ago.

Man, she was funny! Gussied up in this torn flowered robe with a flannel shirt over it. She was cooking something. Can you imagine? It was two in the morning for God's sake. She must have been about fifty . . . gray hair sticking out of her head like starched pins. Her face was a mass of wrinkles . . .ugly old pill. There were dogs and cats all over the damn place. You've seen her walking her pets. A real character. Always smiling and saying hello to everyone. Yeah. That one. In the blue coat. Well, I'll bet she's not smiling anymore!

How about another beer?

The imagined scene infuriated her. She felt alone and helpless in an indifferent world.

What kind of God would let so much evil go unpunished? She had done nothing to cause such abuse, nothing at all. All her life, she had gone out of her way to help other people. She suffered for others and reached out to comfort them. How could anything so unfair happen to her? She was the victim of a cruel twist of fate. If her light hadn't been on, he probably would never have bothered her.

She thought again about her visit to the hospital. She recalled the cold, bare room and the impersonal staff. Why hadn't one single person touched her arm or even asked her name? She was nothing but a routine beating, one of dozens they saw every night.

Well, she couldn't do anything about her attack. It was history. But she could do something about that frigid isolation she felt in the emergency room. She could be there when they brought in another victim. She could comfort and understand. She could respond to the frustration, the hurt, the confusion, because she felt it, too. She knew she could help others who suffered as she had. . . and she promised herself she would try.

She decided to give life another chance.

The final nightmare was over . . . so she thought.

She was on duty when the call came in. The head nurse summoned all the staff and volunteers to the front desk. "That was Highway Patrol," she said. "A chartered bus collided head on with a semi when he tried to avoid a pedestrian. We're the closest hospital. The injured will be arriving any minute. Most of the passengers are suffering from shock and minor lacerations. As they come in, wheel them to the left and line them up. Keep them calm and warm. A doctor will examine them as soon as possible.

"Both drivers have pretty serious injuries, especially the one in the truck. He had a skull fracture and both arms are severed. The worst case is the pedestrian. He was hit head on by the semi and his ribs are crushed. He has serious head lacerations and his leg is just about off. The medics are doing what they can but unless we get him in the operating room right away, he'll probably die from gangrene and loss of blood.

"The minute he arrives, wheel him over to that room on the right. We're getting ready for him right now."

She lined up with the rest of the rescue team at the emergency entrance. One by one, the ambulances pulled into the drive. She blinked at the flashing lights and felt a familiar clutch of fear. She could not steel herself to the sights and sounds of mutilation without reliving her own.

The siren's screams accelerated as two more emergency vehicles roared up to the door. Another siren split the air. The lights of the speeding emergency vans illuminated the frantic movements of the hospital rescue operation as if it were noon. The cries of the injured were a dissonant countermelody to the terse commands of the medical team as they skidded their gurneys through the mud. Those victims who could walk helped one another through the sudden downpour that erupted from an angry sky.

She ignored her own anguish and plunged into the rescue operation. She wheeled one shock victim after another to the left wall. She remembered how alone and ignored she felt that day almost a year ago when she entered those same sliding doors. She paused to give each patient a special word of comfort before she hurried back to the entrance.

She helped one woman to a bench in the waiting room. The victim stared straight ahead, seeing nothing. The tears poured down her face but the woman was too numb to wipe them away. She paused and pulled some tissues from a box. She stuffed them into the other woman's hands and smiled. "I'll be right back," she said and squeezed the woman's hand. It felt cold, damp, as if it had just been removed from a refrigerator.

A paramedic grabbed her. He pointed to a covered gurney. "That's him," he said. "That's the guy who was hit by the truck. Poor fella. He's just about done for. I can't even see him breathing. Can you?"

She looked at the inert form and shook her head. She could feel her eyes fill with empathy. She grabbed the gurney. "I'll handle this one," she said. "We're all ready for him."

She looked down at her cargo. He moved and the sheet slipped from his face. For an endless moment, she stared at the injured man. Behind his mask of pain, she recognized that same cold expression, the same features she still saw when she tried to sleep . . . his face. Once again, she felt remembered pain. She tasted the warm rivulets of her own blood. She smelled the sweet floral perfume that haunted her still.

He opened his eyes and looked at her. She watched his tortured mouth form a word.

"You."

His eyes glazed. He was unconscious.

"Hey," shouted the doctor on duty. "Has that multiple injury gotten here?"

She could feel her heart whack her ribs and she could hardly breath. She swallowed and gripped the gurney. She wheeled it to the left. "No, doctor," she called. "Not yet."

Justice is truth in action.
- Disraeli

Marvelous Mondays

Reading: this polite and unpunishable vice;
This serene, life-long intoxication.
- Logan Pearsall Smith

My love affair with books began the day I was born. My mother bought me a 12-volume set of literature called MY BOOKHOUSE FOR CHILDREN. I taught myself to read in those books and they taught me to think. They were the first things I opened when I awoke and their stories the last thing I heard before I slept. Indeed, it was the content of those pages that showed me the immense potential that life offers us all.

I was not the kind of child who enjoyed playing outdoors. My co-ordination was poor and my sense of competition didn't exist. I didn't like to play games because I never realized the thrill of winning. But I did understand the delight of a happy ending. I knew the heartbreak that tragedy could bring and never could satisfy my thirst for a good story, well told.

When I was small, my flight from peers I could not understand lay between the pages of the books my mother had bought for me. As I grew older, I sought consolation for my unhappiness in those books as well. I became the person I am today because of what I learned in the millions of volumes I have read throughout my life. Although I have hundreds of books in my home, I discovered most of the books that influenced my taste in reading in The Public Library.

I can still remember that magnificent day when I was seven years old and my mother and I boarded a streetcar to see the dedication of the main branch of the Toledo Public Library. We walked together through its doors and up the stairs to the children's room. I gasped when we reached the top of those stairs. I knew that I had ascended to paradise. There were countless shelves filled with thousands and thousands of books. "Someday, when you are bigger, you will be able to come down here all by yourself, Lynnie Ruth," said my mother. "But until then, you will have to settle for the books they have at Kent."

Kent Library was a small branch library on the corner of Collingwood and Central Avenue. It was too far for a seven year old to walk, but such a short car ride that my mother never minded dropping me off there on her way to do her shopping on Monday afternoons.

Oh those glorious Mondays! I gathered the three books I had devoured the past week and walked into a place stuffed with treasures yet to be discovered. It was during those years, I met a little boy named Rufus M and I had my very first experience with Betsy, Tacy and Tibb. I read about a mandarin who lived in a garden of oranges and I cried for a sparrow whose tongue was cut because he sang his song at the wrong time in the wrong place. In what seemed like an instant, my mother tapped me on the shoulder and said, "Have you found the books you want to take home, Lynn Ruth?"

I handed her ten books with tears running down my cheeks. "I just can't choose!" I wailed.

"Well then, we'll just take these three on top and you can get others next Monday," my mother said, and I smiled once more.

Of course! All I had to do was wait for the next marvelous Monday and once more I could choose brand new books to be my companions for the week.

When I was eight years old, and my sister took up most of Mother's time, I learned to walk to the library from Fulton School and make my way home after I had carefully chosen the week's reading. It was a long walk for little legs, well over two miles, but it seemed like inches to me because it was my journey to happiness. By the time I was in the sixth grade, I had read every book in that branch library and as I was starting to re-read some of the really good ones, the librarian said to me, "You know, Lynn Ruth, you are old enough to take the streetcar down to the Main Library all by yourself, now."

I shook my head. "I don't think my mother would ever let me do a thing like that," I said.

"I'll talk to her," said the librarian.

My mother believed that my reading kept me from learning skills I really needed in life, like jumping rope, roller skating and riding a two-wheeled bicycle. She didn't like my indoor pallor and she objected to the paucity of friends who came over to our house to play. I knew very well she would do nothing to encourage my addiction.

I cannot imagine what that librarian said to her, but the next thing I knew, I had my books in a sack and a penny in my hand as I waited for the Cherry Streetcar to take me to the magic building I had seen dedicated six years ago. I pushed open those immense doors and walked up the very stairs I still remembered into a feast of books on shelves that reached to the sky.

My home was not a peaceful place for me. But no matter how turbulent the storms at our dinner table, no matter how angry my mother was at my inability to do her bidding, I could always find a safe corner to curl up with a book. I can still remember creeping into the hall closet, turning on the light and sitting quietly reading a mystery about Nancy Drew or learning about a delightful nurse named Cherry Ames. I could hear my mother's strident voice calling LYNN RUTH! Where ARE you?" and I would hunch down further into my corner, my eyes glued to the lines on the page. Here I am in a hospital helping all the sick patients, or meeting a shy little girl just like me who learned to laugh when she visited her happy cousins.

When I finished the book, I crept out of the closet to cope with Tuesday until Sunday. Then, I boarded the streetcar, handed my penny to the conductor and glowed as if I had an appointment with an angel. "Will you tell me when we get to Michigan Street, please?" I asked.

"Going to the library again, Lynn Ruth?" he said.

"How did you know?" I asked. "I'll bet you guessed because I am carrying all these books!"

"No, no!" said the conductor. "I can tell by the stars in your eyes!"

People say that life's the thing,
But I prefer reading
- Logan Pearsall Smith

The Melting Pot

At the touch of love, everyone becomes a poet
- Plato

My mother's family came to Toledo, Ohio from Yasse, Rumania in 1900. My grandma had lived in a hut with a dirt floor and you can imagine how thrilled she was when my grandpa presented her with the white frame house he had built for her. It had wooden floors, a big front porch with a glider and a real icebox in the kitchen. My grandma bought her groceries in shops run by immigrants like herself and spent the rest of the day keeping house. She spoke Yiddish and that's the language my mother learned.

When my mama entered kindergarten, my grandma bundled her into thick woolen underwear that rumpled around her ankles and a loose dress with a bow at the back. Her hair was combed into long curls tied with a huge ribbon. She smiled at her new teacher and greeted her in Yiddish.

In those days, teachers made no effort to understand the language of the immigrant children who entered their classrooms. It was the child's responsibility to speak the national language. No one encouraged my mother to be proud of her ethnic heritage. Instead, she felt ignorant and confused. And so the worst happened. My mother flunked kindergarten.

Her shame was immense. Somehow, she managed to master the language enough to pass the first grade and by the time she was a teenager, she dressed like everyone else in her class and there wasn't a trace of the old country in her words. Still, she was humiliated by the different way her family lived and the strange foods they ate. She swore that when she had a child, that child would look like children in the magazines she read and it would speak faultless English. It would eat the American Way; no spicy Eastern European stews drenched in chicken fat and reeking of garlic on her plate. My mother's child would go to bed at seven and lunch on tuna fish and mayonnaise, because she was American.

I was that child.

My mother dressed me in starched Shirley Temple dresses and polished Mary Jane shoes. I wore slender leggings and a fitted navy blue coat with a white velvet collar to protect me from the elements. The finishing touch to my outfit was a classy little hat with a white feather that bobbed as I walked. . . a far cry from rumpled woolen underwear and that shapeless dress that hung in uneven lengths somewhere in the vicinity of my mother's knees.

I drank orange juice for breakfast and finished my homogenized milk at every meal. I ate my salads on a separate plate and could not touch dessert until I finished my vegetables. I was not allowed to lisp or slur my words. I never heard baby talk and I certainly never heard Yiddish . . .except at my grandma's house.

When I was three years old, my parents took a month's vacation in Miami Beach. They left me with my grandma. I adored my bubbie. That was what I called her in my perfect American diction. She called me Leenie Root.

The minute my Mama kissed me good by, my grandmother took me into the house and opened up the trunk where she kept my mother's old clothes. She swaddled me in my mother's woolen underwear and topped it with a pink, shapeless dress that had patches at the elbow and hole right near the hem. I thought it was beautiful because it smelled like my bubbie to me. My grandma folded up my Shirley Temple dress and wrapped it in mothballs. "It's too cold to wear such a t'ing in vinter,"she said. "Now, come. I will comb your hair."

She stood me on a chair next to the sink and formed long curls on my head with a wet comb. She tied them back with a great big ribbon and showed me my reflection in her hand mirror. I was thrilled. I looked just like the picture on the mantle of my mama and all my aunts.

How can I ever describe the magic of that month? I woke up each morning to a breakfast of hot oatmeal smothered in sweet butter and syrup and then downed a large cup of baby coffee (1% coffee, 99% milk.) At lunch I ate corned beef or pickled herring with raw onions. I smelled just like my mama did before she left home and learned about halitosis.

Every afternoon, my grandma told me stories about my mama and her three sisters. After dinner, she scooped me up on her lap and we practiced a special American surprise for my mother.

On the day my parents returned, Mama ran up the steps of her childhood home with her arms outspread. "Lynnie!" she cried.

I looked at the tanned stranger who smelled of expensive perfume and I shrunk behind my bubbie's skirt. "Who dat?" I whispered.

My mother looked at me and tried to hide her horror. I stood before her, my rumpled underwear sagging around my ankles, my muslin dress stained with mustard and hot pastrami. My hair was pulled back in long curls. I smelled like a delicatessen and I looked exactly like she did when she was that tormented child frightened by a hostile, new world.

My grandma patted me on the cheek and said. "Sing, Leenie Root. Sing for you mama."

I knew exactly what to do. Hadn't we rehearsed this little routine every evening for a month? I threw back my shoulders, opened my mouth wide and I sang: "Yankee Tootle vent towndown, a ridin' on da po-o-ony!"

And my mother wept. "Oh, Mama" she cried. "How could you do such a thing?"

My grandma lifted me into the air and kissed both my cheeks. "Dat vas gorgeous, Leenie Root," she exclaimed and I can imagine the look she gave my mother over the top of my head. "You sang chust like Jeannette MacDonald!"

Today, we know something my own mother never understood. We know that America is richer for its variety. We don't hold a child back because he can't speak understandable English. Instead, we have special teachers to help that child communicate with others and I think that's a very good thing.

I am very proud of the progress women have made in this century, but I sometimes wonder at the price we paid. My grandma was an uneducated housewife who couldn't read and never dreamed of a life outside her home, but she was never too busy to love a child. Growing up can be a very frightening thing and it is reassuring indeed to know that, no matter how life batters you, in one beloved heart, you are always a treasure.

A child is fed with milk and praise
- Mary Lamb

AUTHOR'S NOTE: This story appeared in the original THOUGHTS WHILE WALKING THE DOG, but it bears repeating. We must never forget the insatiable thirst our children have for our love. If we do not satisfy it, they will never learn to give it. That would be a terrible loss for us all.

Miracle in a Marigold

Illness is the night side of life.
- Susan Sontag

It had been such a long winter, cold and unforgiving. Now it was April; still so cold and bleak, I had ceased to believe in spring. And then, I saw it.

A marigold bloomed on my windowsill.

It was a miracle, that bit of golden sunshine that pierced the gloom outside. Such a thing could never have happened, had it not been for those everyday wonders that bless us all the time. It took the magic of earth and sun, air and water to bring my marigold to life.

Until a few years ago, I never noticed those miracles. Then, on a day far darker than I believed possible, they were taken from me. I was confined to a hospital room and did not leave it for six long months. My bones were losing calcium so rapidly that the doctors feared they would soon crumble.

While I was undergoing interminable tests, I came to know the patients who shared my hospital corridor. It was these people who taught me about the miracles we can make happen because we want them so very much.

Joanne Hawthorne had such high blood pressure the doctors told her she could never survive giving birth. She ignored their predictions and determined to have a baby. She delivered a healthy little boy and has mothered him through his school years. He is a college graduate now, and she will soon become a grandmother. A miracle.

Mr. Livingston was a brilliant lawyer with his future before him. When cerebral palsy crippled him, it destroyed his hopes for a healthy life. He decided to undergo an experimental operation and take the chance that he could maintain his balance to walk once again. After the surgery was performed, his physician told him it was a failure. Mr. Livingston disagreed. Every day he hobbled down that corridor forcing his legs to hold him and his body to maintain its balance. His determination not only carried him down that hall, if took him out of the hospital back to his chosen profession. Another miracle.

Father Michael's blood was so thick with cholesterol it refused to move through his veins. He came to this hospital every year to have his fat filled blood exchanged for healthy serum. Each year, he brought materials to tat a rug he designed for the sisters who cared for him during the year. By the time his medical procedures were completed, Father Michael had finished his rug and his new blood gave him the gift of life for another year.

Yes, that was a miracle for him. But it was one Father Michael didn't notice. He was enchanted by a far greater miracle: the work of art he had finished. "I've never done one creative thing before this," he said. "Yet, every year, I bring something I designed to life. It's a miracle."

At the end of six months, I decided to leave that hospital. The medical staff there still had not found the cause of my calcium loss. "You must not walk outside unprotected," cautioned my doctor. “You risk spontaneous fractures that will never heal."

"I cannot bear locking myself away from the world this way," I replied. "I want to walk outside while I still can."

When I left that hospital, I weighed 55 pounds. My legs looked like matchsticks and no one but me believed I would see morning, much less walk outdoors again. In the years since I returned home, I have never let a day go by without walking in that world of mine. My eyes drink the coppers and reds of autumn as if they were fine wine. Winter's snow thrills me anew each time it carpets the earth. Summer is so lush to me, I cannot bear leaving it to go inside my house. And spring? Every spring is a rebirth for me. It promises hope for another year of discovery in a world I almost lost.

That marigold reminded me that my season of hope had arrived once more and I realized I had never noticed the real wonder of it all. Marigolds will always appear whenever spring arrives. I have welcomed more than thirty springs and thousands of flowers since I left that hospital and my legs still carry me wherever I want to go.

Yes, a marigold appeared on my windowsill that gray April day and it was a wonder to behold. I was so enchanted by it that I failed to recognize the real miracle: I was there to see it bloom.

Life is not merely being alive, but being well.
- Martial

Another Dream

When we lose the right to be different,
We lose the privilege to be free.
- Charles Evans Hughes

Martin Luther King shared his dream of equality for us all, one hot summer day in 1963 and we have come a long way toward making that dream come true. But in our zeal to bestow equal opportunity on all mankind, I wonder if we have compromised another inalienable right: the privilege to be different.

I will never forget another even hotter summer day in 1980, in Wimberley, Texas, peopled by out of sync angels who rejected conformity because it insisted they wear shoes. All of us loved to sing Bible songs, share potluck dinners created from found items and work to make our world a happy place. Not one of us fit any stereotype known to man and none of us cared.

I was housed in a fifth wheel trailer on a ranch just outside of town. I fed two horses and a donkey for the owners of the place in exchange for hooking up to their utilities and using their laundry facilities. I lived with two dogs, one cat and an exhausted air conditioner, barely able to move air much less cool it. The heat that summer was so intense that clothes became a distressing liability. I elasticized a light blue, flowered pillowslip and wore that as a survival measure when the two dogs and I walked the country roads. Every morning, Mark Croy would knock on my door and say, "Hey, Lynn Ruth! " which meant: "Put on your shoes honey, it's time to get going."

Mark was in his early twenties, well over six feet tall and I am just an inch over five feet. Mark wore a ragged straw hat he found in the dumpster outside K-Mart, no shoes and jeans that had seen better days on shorter legs. I was decked out in a fresh pillowslip and tennies. We were often mistaken for Ed Sullivan's Old Gold pack and matches before they got dressed for their commercial.

As we walked, we discussed the remote possibility of a breeze coming our way, the inequalities of rich and poor and where Mark could sleep that night. We turned to the right on the main road and stopped at Martha and Jonah's place for some sun tea and a dip in the stream while we pondered the immense changes in weather that had taken place over the century and marveled that all the birds weren't roasted. Mark swung high in the air in the tire that hung from the oak tree out front and Martha showed me how she had created a loaf of bread out of a yogurt starter, alfalfa seeds and ground acorns. We buttered the crumbling slices with honey from Jonah's hive and washed it down with sassafras tea.

Martha would say how lucky Mark was that his underwear was intact because his jeans were in tatters and Mark would reply that he preferred a breeze through his legs in heat like this. That inspired another round of tea, more seed bread and speculation on God's plan for the Texas hills since it had been months since a breeze had been detected anywhere at all.

Martha and Jonah called their dog Biff and we all continued toward town until we came to the Blue Hole. "Let's take a dip in the quarry," Mark would say and down we would climb to the only place in town where we could cool off.

As soon as we descended, Mark jumped into the quarry and Rachel McGinnis poured pump water over my head to relieve me. I shook the drips from my shoulders and went inside to Luke and Becky stories they refused to believe about midwestern snow storms. As soon as the children's eyes drooped, Rachel kissed them good night and Mark joined me to go back to the main road with Martha, Jonah, Rachel and her husband Abraham. When we hit the main road, we hitched a ride with Mary Lou Redd who drove large expensive cars and did the books for her daddy in San Marcos, the biggest town near us. Mary Lou had a daughter named Shauna who was so beautiful she didn't have to do anything but stand on a corner to attract men faster than flies swarm toward butter. Mary Lou also had a son no one discussed and three immense white dogs known for their determination to catch the moon even in sunlight. She dropped us off at the Sunset Market to get provisions and went home to work her crossword puzzles. "You coming to church later?" I called and she shook her head. "We're Methodists," she explained.

Mark and I bought what we thought we could carry and then continued until we got to the post office where old Mrs. Atlee sat sorting what mail there was and putting it into post office boxes. As soon as we entered the door, her face flooded with smiles and she stood up, hugged us both and gave the dogs fresh bowls of water. "Ain't it HOT?" she exclaimed and we nodded. She opened her fridge, poured us some iced tea (chamomile) and pointed to a platter of blueberry muffins that still had the aroma of the oven about them. "Fresh this morning," she would say. "Y'all just help yourselves," and we all did.

The rest of the afternoon varied from visits to Belinda's Beauty Shop to trim the hair from the all our eyes including the two dog's, to stopping at the Health Emporium for a sprout sandwich and more liquid to wash away the heat inside us. If it was Monday, Wednesday or Sunday, we all gathered in a condemned warehouse that we called church to sing and love each other. If it was Saturday, we went over to the girls' camp to watch outdoor movies. The Drive In was owned by two women who lived in a log cabin behind the big screen and kept two horses in their living room. "I don't like them rooting around in all that grit out back," explained Cassandra Stark. "This way, we got control."

The movies were reruns of old forties films and that year I saw Yankee Doodle Dandy, Random Harvest, and Gaslight twenty three times. We also saw Going My Way, but only once.

On Tuesdays, we all went on a hayride out at Christopher Murphy's farm and on Thursdays we did choir practice. That always puzzled me. "Who listens to the choir?" I asked Martha. "It seems like were all in it."

" I guess the Lord is the one who listens to us," said Martha. "What do you think?"

I didn't answer that one; I just threw back my shoulders, prayed my pillowslip would stay in place while I sang. "AMAZING GRACE!!!!" we roared and indeed our grace was heady wine for us all. Every singer's melody blended together to produce the most thrilling music I have ever heard. Together, we showed the rest of the world the immense difference one person's song can make in the quality of life's chorus. I was in that choir twenty-one years ago and the music we made that summer replays in my heart whenever I forget that each of us is a gift to the universe, a gift that makes the entire world an exciting place for us all.

What one man can do is
Change the world and make it right again . . .
Ain't it great what one man can do?
- John Denver

Nettie Alsop and Martin Luther King

All of us have the right to equal opportunity to develop our talents.
- John Kennedy

Martin Luther King Day always makes me think of Nettie Alsop and how much she would have benefited from the fruits of his lovely dream. Nettie Alsop was my mother's maid in 1939 when I was 6 years old. I loved her so much that I still get tears in my eyes when I realize that she is gone.

Nettie cleaned our house, cooked our dinner and treated me like a precious treasure. Because she had a deformed foot, she walked on crutches but that didn't seem to slow her down. When I was in trouble or a pot boiled over on the stove, she moved faster than a track star.

She was the kind of person who could see a child's invisible pain and cure it with a hug or a story and a walk to the park. No matter how busy she was, she had time to tell me stories and sooth my fears. When she held my hand, the world became a beautiful place. I can remember when I had chicken pox and only she could make the itching go away.

Nettie lived with her sister Carrie in the Brand Whitlock Homes, a housing development for blacks in Toledo, Ohio. Brand Whitlock must have been a man with great vision and understanding because he believed that if you give people decent housing they will enhance the property and he was right. Those brick units became a thing of beauty nestled in the heart of Toledo's worst slum.

Nettie had to quit school when she was twelve because her family needed money and the income she could provide. She took in sewing and her needlework was so precise, it would win prizes if she were showing it today. She read so many books that she knew the answer to every question I ever asked. She was not just intelligent. She was wise. She taught me to understand my playmates and not waste my energy hating those that hurt me. "All they want is a little attention and a little love," she'd say to me. "That doesn't cost a thing to give, and when you make someone feel important, he won't be afraid to be nice to you."

I asked Nettie why she was on crutches and she explained that when she was a little girl like me, she was riding her bicycle and a car hit her. "Didn't they take you to the hospital?" I asked.

Nettie nodded. "My parents rushed me to the emergency ward but the doctors must have been very busy that night and they didn't have time to set a black child's leg."

I couldn't believe what I heard. "But your leg was broken," I said. "They HAD to fix it."

Nettie shook her head. "Not if you were black," she said and she wiped the tears from my eyes. "But it all worked out just fine, Lynnie Ruth," she said. "I learned to run as fast as the next one and I'll bet if you raced to the corner right now, I'd win."

I don't think a terrible injustice like that could happen today, although many of my black friends tell me I am wrong. I don't believe we use color as a criteria when we select our friends or judge their character and it I thank providence that it is illegal now to deny medical treatment to any human being.

When I was young, we defined neighborhoods by the ethnicity of their residents but today, anti-discrimination laws won't allow such a thing. A young lady at San Francisco State once asked me if I lived in a mixed neighborhood and when I finally forced her to explain what that meant, I told her in all honesty that I didn't know.

Tony Bolivar, my town's beloved postman and musician and I share a dream that is as optimistic as Martin Luther King's. We wish that all the races in the world could be dumped in a bowl and mixed together until everyone's skin was creamy beige. Then when a tiny eight year old with a broken leg was taken to a hospital with tears in her eyes, she would be treated like the treasure that all children are. She would have her leg put into a cast so that she would be skipping rope in six weeks and running to her classes at some a college campus by the time she was eighteen. She wouldn't have to sew to earn her living unless that was what she longed to do.

Yes, if Tony and I had our way, everyone could have the right to create reality out of their own vision in life. I guess that's what Martin Luther King wanted, too.

I have a dream that my four little
children will live in a nation
Where they will not be judged
by the color of their skin,
But by the content of their character.
- Martin Luther King

Providence Provides

The smile is the beginning of love
- Mother Theresa

Her name was Maggie. She was part of my life for such a short time that I would think she was only a mirage if I didn't have the little wooden napkin ring she gave to me when I returned from Scotland. I use it at every meal and I remember her.

She appeared on my doorstep as if by magic one April morning in the late eighties. I will never forget my surprise when she rang the bell and told me she heard I needed someone to clean my house. "I've never cleaned house before," she said. "But it couldn't be any different than keeping up my own place. I'd like to give it a try."

I looked at this tall, willowy girl, her fresh scrubbed skin kissed by the sun. Her blond hair was gathered in braids and her bright gingham dress was covered with an apron that looked like a replica from the 18th century. She reminded me of an illustration for LITTLE WOMEN and when she spoke, the cadence of her words sang a hymn to the simple life, the antiquated values of a Quaker community.

"How did you know I needed someone?" I asked. "I was going to start calling the newspaper ads tomorrow."

"I just knew," said Maggie.

"Housekeeping is dirty, difficult work," I told her. "Wouldn't you prefer to do something that gets you outdoors a bit more or challenges your mind?"

"I need to earn money fast," she said. "Bill and I want to take the children away from this artificial, money hungry place and buy some land up north. I don't want them to go to school here and I am sick with worry that they'll start doing marijuana or forget about basic values like industry and charity"

She took my hand and I knew before she spoke again that I would hire her just to keep her with me. "Cleaning up after one person is nothing compared to the mess in my house," she said. "Besides, I like to help people. My master's degree is in social work. I worked in a hospice for a while and I loved it. After that, I was a home nurse and that was okay, but I can't stand taking money from people who are dying. It doesn't seem right."

"Well, I'm not dying," I said. "And my house is filthy. How much do you charge?"

"Whatever you pay," she said.

And that was how our relationship began. In that brief span when I knew her, I never thought of Maggie as my employee. I was often her mentor and always her friend. We went for walks together with her two children, and we traded experiences that gave us both renewed insight into the limitless possibilities in life. We frequented museums and galleries and went to outdoor picnics and concerts. She became family and her presence never failed to enrich me.

I had lived alone for over forty years and when I moved into my own house in Pacifica, I had no support system in place to help if anything disabling happened to me. In an apartment building, there is always the person down the hall and when you rent, eventually the landlord will call. My house is on a quiet street where neighbors mind their own business. Although I had lived on this block for three years, I still did not know the telephone number of the woman who lived with her husband on the east side of my house. The woman on the west had a large family that was often drunk and always angry at my barking animals. I certainly couldn't ask her for help.

As I look back on the sequence of events that followed Maggie's entrance into my life, I cannot help but believe that some higher power sent her to me to see me through the summer. The previous August, I attended the Edinburgh Festival in Scotland. I took every cent I saved from January until July and blew it all on airline tickets, accommodations and a schedule of plays and concerts. This summer, I planned a return and all the arrangements had been made before that April day that Maggie came to me. I would leave August 8th and stay until Labor Day.

The last week in July, I hurried out to water the backyard flowers and as I reached for the faucet, I tripped on the hose and fell against the stucco wall of the house. I sunk to the ground, overwhelmed with pain. I couldn't move; I couldn't even cry for help and I think I lost consciousness because the next thing I knew I heard Maggie's voice. "Lynn Ruth! Where are you? I was in the neighborhood and I decided to drop by with some apple butter I made last night. Lynn Ruth!"

And she was at my side. She lifted me up and took me to the emergency ward of the hospital. I glanced at the clock as we left the house. Maggie had arrived less than ten minutes after I fell. How had she known I needed her?

Four hours later, I was in a plaster cast in my own bed. I had broken my shoulder and cracked the two bones in my upper arm. I couldn't cook my dinner, take a bath or walk any farther than the bathroom. I was an unwilling and furious invalid. "What will I do about Scotland?" I asked the doctor. "I have all the tickets. I can't cancel them now."

"I will give you pain pills," he said. "And I will change your cast right before you leave. We have ten days to get you mobile and I think we can do it if you do your part."

"Count on me," I said.

But I didn't realize that in the next ten days, Maggie's part would be far more challenging than mine.

We never discussed the new demands I made on her time and she refused money for her added responsibilities to me. When I awoke, Maggie was there beside me. She cleaned me up, fed me and settled me in my bed with a good book before she left to take care of her other clients. She was back at six to check up on me and prepare my evening meal. At ten o'clock, she returned to my house in her pajamas, settled me in for the night and left. When she was with me, I exercised my fingers, tried to move my arm and laughed at her jokes. Maggie and I always had fun together.

August seventh the two of us returned to the doctor. "I can't think of a better way to wait out the remaining four weeks of healing than listening to concerts and seeing plays," he said.

"Neither can I," I said.

Maggie got me on the plane and off I went for three weeks of culture. I managed during those days away from home to exercise my arm, learn to re-use the torn muscles and injured in the fall and, on Labor Day, I walked down the gangplank to meet Maggie on my own. She drove me home to an immaculate house, a filled refrigerator and dinner ready on the table. She had purchased a special floral placemat for me with a matching napkin drawn through a cheerful kitten-shaped napkin ring. She painted an immense sign she decorated with butterflies and flowers. WELCOME HOME, LYNN RUTH it shouted on the banner across my door.

The next day I managed to cook for myself and drive to the market slowly. "I have some news," said Maggie. " I can help you this week . . but after that . . ."

She took my hand. "Bill and I found some property outside Yreka and we will be moving there next Sunday."

My eyes filled with tears for losing her mingled with happiness for a step I felt she needed to take. I squeezed her hand. "I'll manage," I said. "Will you write to me?"

"I'll telephone," she said. "I'm a terrible letter writer."

But she didn't call. She left that Sunday and I never saw her again. My shoulder still ached but I could take care of myself. I found someone else to clean my house that did just that and nothing else; and I longed for the sweet presence that had been so inspiring to me. I missed her, but I no longer needed her.

Maggie! Without her, I would have been hospitalized and alone. With her, I was able to continue my life. But when the time came to once more take care of my own needs, she was gone. Perhaps Providence sent her on to someone else who was in trouble. I like to think that happened. And I like to believe her example taught me an important lesson about the reason we are all on this earth together. Because of my memory of her, I try to be a Maggie whenever I can. If I hear a cry for help, I am there. If I see hunger, I feed it. That is my way of saying thank you to Maggie. I like to think that she knows what I do for others and that she is the reason that I do it with so much pleasure.

Necessity is not a fact but an interpretation
- Friedrich Nietzche

The Embezzler

What man was ever content with one crime?
- Juvenal

"This is the last time I'm going to cover for you, Matt," John Arbuckle said. "I realize your financial situation, but I'm the one who has to explain why the company paid $1,000.00 to a Sam Wren and Sons when there is no such account on our books."

Matt Green gripped the arm of his chair. His face was lined with worry. "Please, John," he said. "Just give me until the end of next week. I had to borrow from the company this time. My credit everywhere is used up and Delores had all that emergency dental work last month."

"Matt, the accountants are coming to check our books Tuesday. That means I can give you until Monday, but no longer." He put his hand on Matt's shoulder. "I'm sorry, Matt."

Matt tried to smile. "Well, at least I have the weekend to figure something out. I swear that if I can just get this fixed up, I'll never use company funds again."

"I know you won't," John said. "And who knows? Maybe something will turn up over the weekend."

Matt shook his head. "It'll have to be a miracle. Well, at least we have the office masquerade party this Saturday night to take my mind off the problem. You're going, aren't you?"

"I wouldn't miss it! Martha and I plan for this all year long. This time, I'm going as Napoleon Bonaparte and Martha as Josephine. What are you and Delores going to be?"

"We didn't fuss this year," Matt said. "I'm going as a Halloween ghost and Delores will be a witch on a broomstick."

"I'm sure you'll fool everyone. No one will guess who you are. Who knows, you just might win one of the prizes."

"Well, that would be the first good news I've had in months," said Matt. "I'll see you at the party."

Matt walked out of John Arbuckles's office and sat down at his own desk. He picked up his pencil and drew dollar signs on his desk blotter as he tried to think. He took out his personal address book and read the names carefully. No help there. He had asked every one of those people to bail him out too many times. He picked up the telephone and then hung it up again. He had no one he could call.

He cleared the top of his desk, put on his coat and nodded to his secretary. "I'll be out for the rest of the afternoon, Laurie," he said. "I have some clients I want to see. Will I see you be at the costume party Saturday night?"

"Oh, yes, Mr. Green! But I bet you never recognize me."

"We'll see about that," laughed Matt and he left the office.

He decided to walk part of the way home instead of taking the bus. `A little fresh air will do me good,' he thought. `Maybe I'll think of a way to get me out of this mess.'

He walked past the high-rise buildings in the center of town into the residential section. As he passed the manicured lawns and trim, well kept homes, he noticed an empty lot with some construction going on. `It looks like someone is building a house right next door to the Eaton's. That's where the party is this year. Look at that huge excavation! They must be getting ready to pour the foundation,' he mused. `Say, I wonder . . . '

He approached the site and sure enough, there was a large area dug out right next to the Eaton home. He walked around the excavation and knelt down to feel the soil. It was quite loose. He noticed bags of cement lined up in one corner, obviously ready to be mixed and poured shortly. He returned to the street absorbed in thought.

His pace accelerated as his mind raced with new ideas. By the time he got home, he had figured out the solution to his financial problems. He smiled with relief as he unlocked the door and hugged his wife. "And how's my honey tonight?" he asked. "Does your mouth feel any better?"

"It's just about healed," said Delores Green as she returned his kiss. "And thank goodness for that. I would have hated to be uncomfortable at the party tomorrow night. How was your day at the office?"

"Not bad," answered Matt. "Not bad at all. I didn't have much to do so I walked home, and I feel just great. You really ought to try walking more, Delores. It clears the brain. In fact, I'm going to take another walk after dinner. I think I'll probably sleep better if I do."

That Saturday night, Matt, wrapped in a voluminous white sheet, escorted Delores, her face painted green and smeared with soot, to the Eaton's home. As soon as the two entered, Matt whispered, "You get yourself settled, honey, while I go to the bar. I want to see who's here."

He walked to the bar. He saw William Shakespeare laughing and talking with a French chorus girl. Right next to them was Napoleon Bonaparte holding a highball. Matt smiled to himself. `I'll just let him get a little more alcohol under his belt and then I'll be ready.' he thought and he returned to the vestibule. He found Delores waiting for him there. He took his wife's arm and walked over to a group of people. "Let's see if we can recognize anyone over here," he said to her.

Delores laughed. "I feel like I'm in some strange dreamland; everyone looks so unreal. " she said. "It's like having all the people from my old story books come to life. Look, honey, Alice in Wonderland is chatting with Sinbad the Sailor and isn't that Louis XIV arguing with Rumpelstiltskin?"

Matt nodded. "It feels like all the books in the library opened up and the characters walked out. I can't be certain who anyone is unless I talk to him. And even then, I'm not absolutely sure."

At about eleven o'clock, Matt noticed that the conversation had become louder and more intense. Adam had fallen asleep in his chair, an empty glass dangling from his arm. Ophelia's white robes were stained with liquor and hors d'oeuvres. Obviously, the guests were beginning to feel the effects of too much liquor on their empty stomachs. "Wonder why Joan hasn't begun serving?" Delores said. "Excuse me, honey. I want to go into the kitchen to see if she needs any help."

"Sure, you go ahead," said Matt.

After she left, he looked around for Napoleon and finally spotted him just as he was walking out to the patio.

"He's playing right into my hands," thought Matt, and he followed him outside.

When he was directly behind the costumed figure, he reached into his pocket and took out a rope. He moved closer, then slipped the rope around Napoleon's neck and pulled as hard as he could. He moved so quickly, his victim had no time to utter a sound. In moments, he crumbled in Matt's arms. "Sorry, John, but it was the only way," Matt whispered as he carried his friend to the excavation next door. He put him down in the far corner of the area where he had dug a six-foot trench Friday night, unseen in the dark, starless night. He covered the body with dirt and smoothed the surface carefully until it blended with the surroundings. "Monday, you'll be entombed in cement, my friend," he said. "And Tuesday, I'll be safe."

He wiped his hands on a rag and hurried back to the party. There was no one in the garden as he crossed the patio and entered the house. He walked over to his wife. "Hi, honey," he said. "Sorry I was gone so long but I got involved in some office business with Roger. He was Tarzan. Did you see us? You know, the costumes this year are amazing. I can't recognize anyone."

"I can't either," said Delores. "I spent most of the time in the kitchen helping Joan after I left you. The lady she hired to help disappointed her at the last minute and Joyce Leonard and I pitched in. Maybe that's why I feel so tired. Matt, my mouth is beginning to ache again. Would you mind terribly if we went home before they award the prizes? You can find out who won Monday."

"Sure, honey. I'm pretty tired too. I think everyone will understand. Let me get our coats."

That night, Matt Green had the first good rest he'd had in months.

The following Monday, he appeared at his desk at nine o'clock. He felt fresh and ready for a new day and a new start on life. He began to sort through his morning mail when he heard someone enter the room. He looked up and turned pale. John Arbuckle walked toward him. "Matt!" he said. "I looked for you at the party the other night. I saw you when I first got there but then you and Delores disappeared. You heard what happened to Sam Walters didn't you?"

"Sam Walters? No. What did happen to him?" Matt tried to keep his voice under control. "I didn't recognize him at the party at all."

"He disappeared. His wife is frantic. You must have seen him! He was Napoleon and I . . . "

"But I thought you were going as Napoleon," said Matt.

"I did, too," answered John. "But at the last minute, Martha found out that the Walters were going as Napoleon and Josephine so she changed our costumes. I was Louis XIV, and would you believe I won the grand prize! Saturday night was really a lucky night for me!"

"It certainly was, John," said Matt. "It certainly was."

When fortune flatters, she does it to betray.
- Syrus

Walking With Perry

Who hears music feels his solitude peopled at once.
- Robert Browning

When Perry Como, that quintessence of The Fifties Crooner died last May, part of me died with him. Although he never knew it, each time I heard his voice reminding me to "Sing, Sing a Song," my voice joined his. But when the two of us swung into that lilting chorus, I doubt that he felt one half the pleasure I did. "I love you a bushel and a peck," was more than a line from a popular ditty to me. It was my loyalty pledge to the man who accompanied me as I walked my way back to health. Although we had never been introduced, Perry Como was my invisible companion for at least two hours every day during the most lonely and difficult time of my life. When he stopped singing his song, I too felt silenced.

In the late fifties, I was fighting a losing battle with anorexia and bulimia. Everyone who listens to talk shows knows that although I thought my hunger was uncontrollable when I binged and I wasn't hungry when I starved, in reality I was trying to kill myself with food. In my case, I tried a few other murder weapons used by the villains in Agatha Christie and Dashiel Hammit novels, as well. However, despite meticulous pre-planning, the rope always broke; the motor stalled, the pills were old and the blade dull. One day, I realized that although I had almost destroyed my body, I couldn't get rid of its central non-disposable item: me. What I had managed to do was make that indestructible me feel lousy all the time. It was definitely time to travel toward a new attitude. I looked in the mirror at the sallow bag of bones I had become and decided there was only one person who could repair that image: the very me I had been kicking around.

How do you undo years of torturing your body and playing mind games with yourself? How do you force yourself to want to feel human again? Those seem like easy questions to answer but in reality they are extremely difficult problems to solve. The obvious way to reverse physical disintegration is to tune up the machine that houses you and recharge motivating forces in your head. This project sent me on one of the more challenging journeys of my life and, while I traveled, Perry was right there reminding me that "Love Makes the World Go Round".

I forced myself into an inflexible schedule to rebuild my body and sweep the cobwebs out of my outlook. I decided to use tools that have been around since the beginning of time: the fresh air that was still plentiful in those days, unprocessed food and exercise. This is how it worked: I got up in the morning.

Now, this in itself was an immense achievement. I was so disillusioned I saw no point in enduring all the pain that involved only to be too weak to accomplish anything until it was time to go back to bed. However, I had made a new set of rules and once made, I determined to follow them. I dressed and cooked an elaborate breakfast that I really ate. This was another gigantic hurdle and I was very proud of myself. It had always been my habit to insist that although I had not eaten since a week ago Wednesday, I couldn't force a morsel of food into my mouth. This time, I chewed and swallowed everything on my plate.

My next challenge was hauling myself out into that fresh air and breathing it. In the late fifties, we didn't have walkmans or earphones and where I lived there weren't even billboards to stimulate my brain. Anyone who took long walks was forced to resort to his own company and during this period of my life, I didn't find my thoughts very uplifting. One day, as I was bracing myself for the barren trip ahead, I heard Perry Como on the radio and in that moment, I forgot my pain. Indeed, I did what I always do when I hear a catchy tune. I sang along.

No matter how depressed I am, music never fails to fill me with immense joi de vivre. I simply cannot resist singing a great melody. "Catch a Falling Star, " said Perry Como. "Put it in your pocket; never let it get away."

I smiled down at my leashed puppy. "Shall we?" I asked and he wagged his tail. I could almost hear him say, "Sounds good to me!""

As the two of us danced down the steps of my mobile home to the rhythm of Perry's song, I remembered another he had sung to me not twenty minutes before I started putting on my wraps. "Don't let the stars get in your eyes," I told my dog and we boogied on down the narrow path to the highway. I passed the mailbox that marked my first mile and smiled at a Ford convertible with a couple sitting very close together. "Hello, young lovers, whoever you are!" I called and when I waved, they waved back.

When my step slowed and I didn't think I could manage to put one foot in front of the other anymore, I gasped, "Send in the clowns!" and in they came, somersaulting and tumbling around in my head to spur me on my journey to well being.

When I fall in love with a song, I have an irresistible compulsion to learn its words. As soon as I returned home, I played and replayed Perry's music on the phonograph so I could remember the lyrics and sing them outside in the cold wind and pouring rain. "You've come a long way from St. Louis," I shouted to the falling snow as I forced myself outside in that series of storms that attack the Midwest without mercy from October until May. "You're not sick, you're just in love," I told myself when I was coughing my way through a case of the flu. "Tie a yellow ribbon round the old oak tree," I demanded when I saw the first tiny crocus force its way through frozen ground.

Any musician will tell you that a good song is far more infectious than the common cold; twice as contagious as scarlet fever. After a few months of solitary outdoor concerts, my songs took on such a happy lilt that their volume reached the intersection six blocks away. The magic of my music was so strong, my neighbors couldn't resist raising their windows when they heard me make my way down their street. They stopped vacuuming the rug, or polishing the furniture and they sang, too. "Somebody up there likes me!" I sang to all those newly opened windows and suddenly I stopped. I looked at the familiar, smiling faces that had been strangers to me only months before and I realized how right Perry Como was. Someone up there likes every one of us enough to fill our lives with joyous song.

Once I figured that out, I began to like me, too.

Guns aren't lawful; nooses give
Gas smells awful; you might as well live.
- Dorothy Parker

December's Occasions

Every day is a holiday because we are in it!
- Lynn Ruth

December is the month of bright lights, twinkling candles and revelry repeated so often it loses its meaning. There is hardly a day in the month that some end of the year event doesn't beckon us to leave work early, put on our prettiest costumes and enjoy. We are invited to open houses, candlelight services, concerts and plays to celebrate the birth of a religion, the beginning of a season, the rescue of a temple and the arrival of another year.

Often in our rush to avoid the holiday crowds, buy endless gifts for each occasion and juggle our calendars to squeeze in every event, we forget that, in reality, December is the time to be thankful for the most precious gift we all are given at birth: life.

I have always felt that people born in December are cheated of a proper birthday celebration because their friends and family have to cram so much into every day that December babies are lucky if someone manages to scrawl a hurried greeting at the bottom of their annual Christmas mailing, or drop off one gift early to commemorate their place on earth. I, too, was guilty of neglecting my friends born in December, until I met Joan Eck.

It was in 1985, at the War Memorial Opera House. I had driven there from Redwood City in a downpour that would have forced Noah into another ark to hear Pavarotti sing La Boheme. I parked miles away from my destination and sloshed into the Opera House dripping and furious with the perverse elements tried to drown me. I hung my dripping coat in the cloakroom and, I entered the vestibule. My hair sent rivulets of rain down my nose, and when I brushed them away, there she was.

She stood like a sun goddess, immense and shining in glorious costume. Indeed, her very presence rekindled the excitement and grandeur of an opulent night at the opera. She was a very large, blonde woman with eyes that mirrored happiness as natural to her as breathing. She seemed a Technicolor recreation of Woman; her aura was intoxicating and her smile a sunburst.

We bonded instantly and became close friends through the years. As her life story unfolded, I realized she had a past filled with bitter disappointment and shattered dreams. Joanie was a gifted opera singer whose career was amputated by her mother's demands, her own unexpected illnesses and a bad marriage that went sour even before it was a legal document. Those disappointments rolled off her shoulders like raindrops. She would not allow them to dilute her pleasure in the act of living. To me, her being captured the essence of a month when we give gifts to our to those that have enriched our lives because we are so very happy they are part of the universe.

Some years ago, Joanie's eyes began to fail. She had surgery after surgery but nothing could stop darkness from enveloping her. When a child is born blind, it learns to deal with the world with the remaining four senses. Joan Eck was in her sixties when her retina lost its functioning power and she could no longer see her wonderful world. It always seemed to me that one who loved beauty for its own sake, should not be robbed of its presence. Then I realized that Joan never lost her knowledge of the lovely objects that surrounded her even though she did not see them. She still rejoiced in every moment and cherished living her day.

Joan was particularly fond of animals and she would search for gifts to send to my furry family for no special reason except that she remembered how adorable this cat or that dog was when she could see him. She moved to Florida in 1990, almost totally blind. Yet she managed to send me clippings of art reviews, and stories about singers, artists and writers at least once a month to remind me that she was thinking of me. When she sent these clippings, she sent me countless coupons for food, toys, and treats for my dogs and cats.

We wrote until the last when she not only could not see, but had become bed ridden and lame. She died in December not hours from the date she entered this world and a few weeks later, I received a letter telling me she had willed me a lovely set of antique plates that commemorated Shakespeare, the bard who made every phrase a gift to his readers.

Yes, it was Joan Eck that taught me what December is really about. It is about people like this amazing woman who labeled misfortune a challenge and disaster a momentary set back. It is about seeing every day in this month and every other month as a reason to love the people in the world and work hard to make it a charming place for us all to be. At Christmas, I give thanks that I am alive and surrounded by lives that will grow more beautiful and more exciting every day. At Chanukah, I take a moment as I light each candle to extol the unique gifts I have been given by providence and when New Year's Eve rolls around, I blow horns and send out rolls of confetti to express wonder that I have another exciting year ahead to be me.

I cherish December more than any other month in the year because for thirty-one days, everyone celebrates life the way Joan Eck did all year 'round. I hold open my arms to embrace humanity and because it is December, everyone cannot wait to hug me back. "Hooray!" I cry. "I am me! And Hooray again! Because you, my dear friend are YOU.

When we lose the right to be different,
we lose the right to be free.
- Charles Evans Hughes.

The Spirit of Survival

A man's experience of war never ends with the war.
- Anne Michaels

On April 19th, compassionate people throughout the world will light candles to remind them of the holocaust in Nazi Germany. Millions of human beings were exterminated because of one man's lust for power and no one was willing to risk their lives to save them in time. When I think of those who lived through this unimaginable bloodbath and survived to create a better life, I am astounded once more by the limitless ingenuity of the human spirit. My friend Rosalie was born in Germany and her family sent her to Holland at the outbreak of the war. A Dutch family hid her all those dark, forbidding years until the war ended, at last. Rosalie was not one to be crushed by experience. Instead, she used her tragedy to strengthen her resolve to force life to give her the great treasure it can hold for us all. While she was in hiding, she let her imagination create a picture of The Ideal Life and once she was free, she determined to make that life real.

She wanted to marry, have several children and give them the security and love she was denied because of her religion. She chose to live the rest of her life surrounded by beauty and bathed in serenity. She sought comfort, security and freedom from tears. A lot of people long for these things, even those who weren't victims of a racial purge, but very few are willing to take the necessary steps to make them happen. Rosalie was one of those few.

She managed to find an agency to sponsor her passage to New York and when she arrived, she taught herself English by listening to the people speaking around her. She walked into Bloomingdale's Department Store and asked for a job in her broken English. The Personnel Manager listened to the foreign flavor of her speech and decided she could lend a bit of class to the ready-to-wear department, because her accent could easily be mistaken for French. She was hired.

She lived alone in New York for several years and took care of her every need with will power alone. She had no one to interpret her needs to others or help her when she was sick or frightened. She woke up one morning with a pain in her abdomen so wrenching she could barely stand and she dragged herself to a hospital emergency ward before she collapsed. Her appendix had ruptured. Had she waited one hour longer to get help, she would have died.

Death had no place in Rosalie's master plan. She recovered, as she knew she would and continued her department store job until she saved enough money to come out to California. She worked at City of Paris for a while and then The Emporium, gradually inching herself up the couture ladder to become a buyer for the company. Meanwhile, there were other parts of her master plan she needed to put in place. She met a happy-go-lucky mechanic for United Airlines who had also been born in Germany and the two of them married. They had three children and brought them up surrounded by the love, beauty and security the two of them had never known in their own childhood.

Unlike so many other holocaust victims, Rosalie and her husband did not waste time on regrets or aborted opportunities. They concentrated on filling the present with happiness. "I cried enough for ten lifetimes," Rosalie told me once when we shared a cup of tea on her patio in San Carlos. "Now I want to fill my life with laughter."

She did just that not only for herself, but also in abundance for her customers at the Emporium and for her husband and three children. Her quest for the joy spread like a refreshing breeze far beyond the walls of her California home. Rosalie designed beautiful dolls that she exhibited all over the Peninsula. She made them for her children and her grandchildren. She sold them to little children who loved them for whatever their parents could afford because she needed to give those youngsters the happiness that had eluded her until she was able to take her fate into her own hands. This was her legacy to the fates that had opened the right doors for her.

I don't think Rosalie ever realized how much she created her own luck. She believes that the cards fell right for her to live a fulfilling life. But those of us who know her, have a very different picture. We see a woman who has used her very suffering to create compassion for every human being she meets. There is no person I have ever met kinder and more responsive to human need. She and her husband are in their eighties now and have given up their lovely landscaped home in San Carlos where her husband terraced the back yard with layers of flowers and the two of them built their dream brick by brick, inch by inch. Rosalie refused to recognize danger because she, like all true survivors, know that to admit an evil gives it the force to overwhelm you.

"I've had enough of tears", Rosalie told me that day on as we looked out at the view of the cascading hills behind her house. She smiled at me and that smile taught me one of the most important lessons I will ever learn. If a tiny little girl can use that golden fuel to shed the wounds of humiliation and hunger, so can each of us make our impossible dreams real. If one small abused child can summon up the energy of hope and let it propel her across an ocean to build a new life, so can every one of us find beauty in our moments and let them bless all humanity. Indeed, there is a Rosalie within us all if we but search for her in our hearts. It is our magic…that special force that makes our everywhere a paradise.

I must give what I most need.
- Anne Michaels

Spring Laughter

Impropriety is the soul of wit
- W. Somerset Maugham

My lilac bush bloomed this week and its glorious fragrance reminded me of a spring many years ago when I was working with children of holocaust victims in an after-school program at Toledo's Jewish Community Center. Our building with its adjacent playground was located in the inner city and the children gathered there after school to wait for their parents to return from work. Most of the parents could not speak English and although their youngsters attended public school, they had no idea what was being said to them. Although we tried to help these youngsters adjust to their new culture, none of them had a happy time their first few years here.

Their parents struggled to make a living at menial jobs that matched neither their skills nor interests and at night they went to school to learn the new language that was the key to unlock the dreams that had kept them alive during the nightmares they endured. They were determined to give their children a future that would erase the violence they had suffered. I don't think in all my years working with children that I have ever seen a parent hug his child with such fierce and protective love as I saw during that summer of '48.

I remember two of the children in particular. Bella was a squat child, very short for her five years and fat. Hers was not the healthy plumpness of a well-fed child. It was the bloat of malnutrition that welfare meals couldn't alleviate. She was an angry child who pushed the other children if they tried to join her at the sandbox or asked for a turn on the swing. In the several months I watched over Bella, I never heard her laugh even when her parents came to fetch her. She would gallop to them kicking and pushing her way through the collection of other youngsters gathering up their belongings and run into their arms screaming a tirade only the three of them could understand.

In contrast, the other child I remember was a tiny mite named Herschel who came to the playground each day immaculately dressed, sporting an iridescent three-colored skullcap on his head with a propeller on top. Jewish boys from the old country believed in covering their heads and Hershel's Mama wanted her son to preserve tradition and still look like an American child. She had seen other children wearing the spinning propellers and with the very first coins she could spare from those she spent for food for her family, she purchased this American version of a yarmulke for her little boy.

Herschel sat for hours without moving, lost in fantasies I dared not ask to share. His tiny face was always serious and he would often come up to me and slip his hand in mine as if my presence protected him. I picked him up and hugged him, but he, like Bella and all those emotionally scarred children never smiled. There was always sound on that playground: scuffling feet, screams of alarm and the whoosh of children plunging down the slides or swinging high in the air. There was the clatter of lunchboxes, dropped building blocks and bouncing balls. But no laughter. Never any laughter.

At that time, my family owned a feisty terrier named Junior; my cousin Jessica had a dachshund, Pee Wee whose back feet trailed two blocks behind his front paws and the Kaplans had an ebullient collie named Zeke. Down the street, Maureen Zeitz owned a white ball of fluff named Darlene. Maureen pinned a different ribbon in Darlene's hair every night before she took her on a walk around the park. Susan Zarneke had a little Yorkie mix named Beverly who danced on her leash like a ballerina auditioning for Swan Lake.

One spring night as I returned home from the playground, the lilacs were blooming and the ground was covered with swatches of color. Tulips and daffodils lined my path and the fragrance in the air was celestial. As I drank in its beauty, I dissolved into laughter at the antics of my neighbors and their pets in the park on our street. Zeke was chasing Junior while Beverly leapt over and under them and Darlene posed under a dogwood tree. How I wished my little group of children could see this delightful panorama of spring madness.

I called Jessica right after dinner and I told her about the contrast between what I had seen and the gloom that pervaded the Center playground. "I wish I could do something to make them act like children, " I said. "They left one prison only to find another almost as awful for them. There are no gardens in those tenements and none of them are allowed pets. It's really sad."

"Maybe we can convince everyone to decorate their dogs with fancy ribbons or flowers and bring spring to them," said Jessica. "I'll get everyone here to help. We have a station wagon and so does Mrs. Zarneke. If we make it all happen Friday afternoon, the children will have something nice to remember all weekend."

That Friday, I gathered all the children around me on the playground. "Does anyone know what season this is?" I asked.

No response.

I cleared my throat. "IT'S SPRING!!" I exclaimed. "Look!"

I pointed to the street where my aunt and Mrs. Zarneke were parking their cars. The doors of the cars swung open and out jumped Junior, his collar decorated with daffodils and jingling bells. He charged into the sandbox and met Bella on her way to the jungle gym. Bella paused, amazed and then she and our little terrier began a spirited game of tag around the slide, under the swings and into the sand box. Pee Wee waddled over to Herschel. He licked the little boy's foot and the child knelt down and stroked the dachshund's head. Zeke wore a plaid bandana around his neck; a tulip rested behind his ear and lace booties graced his giant paws. He romped into the playground to nuzzle Brendel Schwartz while Beverly leaped and swirled in the air like the accomplished ballerina she thought she was.

"LOOK AT DAT!" screamed Martin Edlebaum and everyone gasped. The back door of our station wagon swung open and out strolled Darlene, dressed as I have never seen a dog adorned before or since. She had simulated white and brown saddle oxfords on each paw with cuffed bobby sox, and a floral cape around her shoulders. She wore a tiny tutu over her hips and on her head was a red straw hat trimmed with daisies. She paused as all well trained models do, surveyed her charmed audience and strolled among the awed children.

The stunned silence was broken by a trill of laughter and soon every child on that playground was giggling and tussling with their new spring friends. I looked at this scene filled with so much audible joy, but I could not join in their laughter. My eyes were blinded with tears.

There is nothing like laughter
to make children bloom.
- Lynn Ruth

The Funny Way That Dreams Come True

We are the music makers
We are the dreamers of dreams.
- Arthur O'Shaughnessy

When I was a child, I believed in wishing on stars. Every night, I stood with my eyes glued to the evening sky and recited a long list of miracles I wanted to happen in my life. It is more than six decades since I began these nightly appeals and to my surprise most of those dreams have actually become reality. The reason I was surprised was that they crept up on me in very unexpected ways.

The very first time I looked up at heaven, I informed my twinkling confidante that I wanted to be a mommy. I wanted to have lots and lots of little children I could care for and love with all my heart. I promised that if my wish came true, I would never raise my voice or strike my babies. Instead, I would play with them and adore them. I would indulge them in sweet desserts and smother them in kisses and bear hugs.

Throughout the years, I added other dreams to my list, but the dream of a loving family always topped the list. I wanted people to read my writing; I wanted to be beautiful; I wanted a date for the Junior Prom. I wanted an A on my history test and I wanted to give something important back to the world.

As I approached my teen-age years, I realized that it took more than a wish to create a family. I needed a man around the house. I needed that man not just to make the babies I wanted to love. I needed him to reach the shelves I couldn't, fix screen doors that dangled from their hinges and doctor the plumbing when it didn't respond properly. My own mother did not have this kind of man in our house and it was a source of constant frustration for her. "Why can't you FIX anything," she would roar at my father when the disposal erupted half ground grapefruit rind sprinkled with coffee grounds and egg shells all over the kitchen floor.

My father would look appropriately baffled and run to the closet for his coat. "I have an appointment with Joe Aronson in twenty minutes, honey," he would say no matter what time of the day or night it was. "I have to hurry or I'll be late."

Although he wasn't handy, my father did the accepted man thing of his day. He trudged out every morning to earn a living for us and when he came home, he hauled heavy cartons out to the trash and walked the dog when it was too dark for nice women like my mother to be outside alone. He always drove the car when we went out as a family and he paid all the bills. He took care of us, but he never played with us and he never contributed one moment to our personal care.

I realized that I wanted a more complete daddy for my family. I needed one that was handy and didn't run away every time I asked him to do fatherly thing. I wanted a whole person who shared the responsibility of all those children I expected to have running around the place; someone who was fun.

As the months turned into years and my life took me across the country, I gave up those fantasies. I stopped wasting my energy wishing on stars for things that weren't going to happen to me and began living the life I had. I realized that it took many men to fulfill the role I had wanted for my all-round companion in life. I discovered that women as well as men could fix things, earn livings and drive when the roads looked bad. No matter where I lived, I could pick up the telephone and within moments get someone help me out when I couldn't cope. I didn't need that dream to come true. There are men aplenty to have around when I want fun, men more than willing to fix the things that break around here and the best part of it is that after they repair the problem, they go home and someone else cooks their dinner, does their laundry and tells them they are never around when they are needed.

But the one dream I really missed was being a mommy. All my other achievements pale when I recall other women my age with children hanging on to their hands as they crossed the street and looking up at them with wonder in their eyes. As the years passed, I envied the thrill on those mother's faces as they recounted all the remarkable accomplishments their children had done and I expressed appropriate amazement. Now, those very same matrons are grandmothers and they are busy baby sitting tiny tots and helping daughters cope with the added responsibilities of the millennium.

Not long ago, someone remarked, "It's fortunate that you don't have children. You could never write your books and paint your pictures if you had that kind of responsibility."

I shook my head. "No," I said and I swallowed the inevitable lump in my throat. "I don't consider it lucky at all."

And then I paused, and I smiled. "Now that I think about it, we're both wrong," I said.

Indeed, I DO have children. They just don't look like the ones I expected to have all those years when I pleaded with those twinkling spirits. Every one of them walk on four legs and I never have to buy them new clothes for school. Although I don't bake them pies and cakes or give them an allowance, I do cuddle them a great deal. The amazing thing is that they have achieved exactly the same triumphs my friends' youngsters have. Over the years, I have had upwards of twenty children and they have all made me very, very proud. I had David, the black fuzzy mutt who walked me back to health and looked both ways before we crossed the street. I mothered Michael Mistake, the little kitten who kept me company when I thought I would wither with loneliness. I adopted Cindy who loved me so much she couldn't sleep unless she had checked my heart and heard its beat, and Molly who believed I had celestial powers because I rescued her from the trunk of an abandoned car. When my friend Mary tells me her Christine is dancing in the Nutcracker, I counter with tales of my Amy, a Yorkie Diva who pirouettes on her toes whenever I sing to her and Dorothy, who specializes in bouncing gymnastics.

I have even had my share of men around this house. I had Max, a sportsman who loved skateboards and Jake, a prince with an Oedipus complex. I had Charles who never stopped being my beloved until he died. Now I have my macho Spaniard, Paul, who refuses to stray one inch from my heel and my little Frenchman, Donald who eyes all the ladies the way all Frenchmen do, but always comes back to me because mine is a love he can count on.

That's a very big family and I assure you I receive far more from them than I ever give in return. They must know that I think they are celestial because I never tire of exclaiming at their beauty, their cleverness, their perfection.

I have many friends who bemoan the unfortunate turns their lives have taken. I always want to put my arms around them and whisper that if they open their eyes, they will realize that everything they have wanted in their lives has happened to them just as it has happened to me. They just haven't noticed their good fortune.

It isn't much of a trick to make dreams come true. The hard part is recognizing them when they do.

Reality only reveals itself
When it is illuminated by a ray of poetry
- Georges Braque

The Little Voice

Laws do not persuade because they threaten.
- Seneca

Michael Woods was a very good boy from Toledo, Ohio. He never was late for school. He obeyed his mother and did not eat between meals. He always said "please" and "thank you" and he kept his pants zipped up tight. He whispered in the library, took his hat off in public buildings and never threw snowballs at children smaller than he.

When he grew up, he followed speed limits and did not litter the streets. He leashed his dogs and picked up their droppings. He shoveled his drive so the neighbors wouldn't slip on the ice when they walked by. He wore a tie and a jacket to work, bathed regularly and never spit.

On his twentieth birthday, he realized he had spent the first two decades of his life obeying a lot of rules made by strangers. He felt like he was living in a prison chained to rigid routines that smothered him. He couldn't think of anything he wanted to do that wasn't against some law somewhere. He was very unhappy.

That was when he left the Establishment and tripped out. He began by smoking pot but it wasn't long before he found a good dealer and started doing cocaine, crack, heroin, opium, and any substance anyone sold him that wrapped him in a soft, insensate cloud. "When I finished my bananas and cream for breakfast," he said, "I smoked the peel."

Other than the occasional evening spent in the gutter, Michael Woods was as happy as a spaced out human being can be. Then one day in the late sixties, a friend told him he discovered a new bar and instead of taking him across town, drove him to a sales meeting in Cleveland, Ohio. Michael Woods remained in his perpetual haze during the entire trip and didn't see light until the speaker appeared on stage. Something about the enthusiasm of the man penetrated his blurred mind and he leaned forward to hear what the man was saying. "YOU CAN DO ANYTHING YOU WANT TO DO!" shouted the speaker. "IF YOU WANT TO RULE THE WORLD OR FLY TO THE MOON, YOU CAN DO IT."

Everybody in the auditorium stood up and clapped their hands. "Hear, hear!" they shouted.

"YOU NEED TO TAKE RISKS FOR SUCCESS," roared the man.

"ARE YOU READY TO TAKE THE FIRST STEP?"

Everyone there jumped up and down and screamed, "YES, YES, YES!"

Michael Woods blinked. He couldn't believe what he saw. There in that auditorium were hundreds of happy people who loved every minute of their lives. "Not one them even smoked cigarettes," he said. "They were high on LIFE."

Michael Woods arrived home very late that night because Cleveland was a three-hour drive from Toledo. He thanked his friend and went into his house. He stuffed every bit of dope, every cigarette, all the booze he had stockpiled and the needles, the alcohol and three flourishing marijuana plants into a plastic bag and threw them into the dumpster on his corner. Then he returned home to dry out.

The next week was a brutal roller coaster of hot flashes, cold sweats, hallucinations and dry heaves but he kept the vision of those happy people before him and he didn't weaken. He slept a little, he vomited a lot and he dreamed magnificent, impossible dreams.

After ten days, he staggered down to his basement and found three 4x8 foot masonite panels he had intended to use to spruce up his recreation room. He dragged them into his dining room and stared at them for a long time. Then he stumbled downstairs once more and found a bag of patching plaster, several cans of spray paint and two dead fern plants he had meant to pitch in the garbage.

He walked outside picked up dead branches, fallen leaves, buckeyes and pine cones, stuffed them in another plastic bag and returned to his dining room to sleep some more. When he awoke, he sprayed one panel black, another blue and another maroon. He took a can of gold paint and sprayed a round circle near the top of the panels and then smeared patching plaster all over the bottom. He stuck all the weeds and branches he had gathered into the wet patching plaster and sprayed it silver and green. Then he opened a can of house paint and spattered it across each painting until it shimmered and vibrated with color. He fell sleep again before he managed to wash his brushes.

He awoke to three beautiful worlds he had created out of nothing but leftover masonite, patching plaster and weeds. "I felt just like God," he said. "And my headache was gone."

He dragged all three panels into his truck and drove to The Avant-Garde Art Gallery on Central Avenue. He approached the woman behind the desk and said, "Wait right there. I have something to show you that you've never seen before."

She removed her glasses and looked at the haggard, filthy young man tracking mud on her new carpet and she frowned. "Wanna bet?" she asked.

Michael Woods walked back outside and dragged in his first masterpiece. He stood it up against the wall and the woman gasped. "I told you," said Michael Woods and he left to haul in the other panels.

"These are fabulous," said the woman. "But they are too big and far too heavy to hang on our walls. Besides they don't have frames."

"Do you like them?" asked Michael Woods.

"I LOVE them," said the woman. "But we have rules for submitting art and specifications about the pieces we hang in our gallery. These panels do not fit our format."

"I see," said Michael Woods and he picked up his artwork and staggered to the door.

"Wait!" said the woman. "I didn't say you should take them away. I just said they don't conform to our standards."

"I never have been good with rules," said Michael Woods

"I see that," said the woman. "That's because you are an Original."

"Is that a good thing to be?" asked Michael Woods.

The woman nodded. "That is the BEST thing to be. Originals are the only people lucky enough to hear their Little Voice."

She rose and took his hand. "Every one of us have a tiny voice inside us that tells us how we need to live, but very few of us pay any attention to what we hear. Instead, we do all the things that are expected of us. If there weren't people like you who listen to that magic voice of theirs, the world would have remained exactly the same since the day it began. You have given the universe a priceless gift."

Michael Woods blushed. "Thank you," he said.

"Ah no, my friend," said the woman. "Thank YOU."

The future belongs to those who believe
in the beauty of their dreams.
- Eleanor Roosevelt

Good News for the Lavendar Girls

I shall go out in my slippers in the rain
And pick the flowers in other people's gardens
AND LEARN TO SPIT
- Jenny Joseph

There is a burgeoning society of women of a certain age, who meet to share their joie de 'vivre over a cup of tea. They wear purple dresses and outrageous red hats and call themselves names like Get Away Gals or Adorable Divas. The only requirement for admission to the sisterhood is The Birthday and that birthday is their fiftieth.

If you dare try to enter their festive ranks before coming of age, you must wear lavender and pink. Now, I have long since passed the lavender stage of my development, but I remember it well. It was a grueling experience for me, filled with failed dreams and shattered hopes. I never realized that those endless disappointments and worries were the bricks and mortar that I needed to build a magic world for myself the day of The Birthday.

I was living in Redwood City at the time in a one room flat so small it would fit inside a disabled toilet stall with room for a small garden in front. My income was $375 a month which I supplemented with a bit of baby sitting and the matchmaking I did for a telephone dating service that offered a money back guarantee. I was most concerned about my future because I knew that my monthly stipend would never pay the rent in a senior care facility if one of my body parts stopped working. During those lean, lavender years, I opened a money market account and religiously sent in every penny I earned above my base income.

Although I spent no money on movies or entertainment, I was rich indeed in pleasures. I borrowed a black skirt and blouse from a sympathetic friend and ushered paying customers to their seats for every event I wanted to see. It was a glorious life filled with opera and orchestras I had only heard on Public Radio. I sang the arias from the previous evening as I trudged to the dating service to fix up sailors with eager ladies willing to give them more than a nightcap. I felt like Pearl Mesta on a mission.

I drove an ancient Valiant that leaked through the trunk whenever a mist floated across El Camino Real and driving it felt more like swimming forty laps to me. Before I could ignite the engine I had to empty it. I bailed out the back seat, blotted the puddles in the trunk and used a siphon I had rigged up with a garden hose to remove the water submerging the brake.

Every month, my friend Jane from the Sisters of the Sacred Heart dropped off a bag of clothes and I refreshed my wardrobe. I was carefree and happy until I went to the grocery store or the gas station. Only then did I realize that I had paid for three advanced college degrees and my economic status was that of a bag lady.

On the morning of The Birthday, a statement arrived from that Money Market Fund I had been filling like a mail order piggy bank. Oh, other statements had arrived from this very obtuse company but they had so many strange figures and columns I couldn't make sense of them. However, in honor of my fiftieth year, they decided to clarify their monthly report to me. I opened the envelope and saw in huge black letters:

BALANCE: $44,000.02

I blinked. I shook my head and took the paper to the window to be certain I was reading it correctly and indeed I was:

BALANCE: $44,000.02

Amazing. That was enough money for a down payment on a house; enough to buy a car, and plenty to buy my very own black skirt and blouse... one that fit. I stared at the piece of paper for a long time. "You know," I told myself. "You could have indulged yourself in one movie. . . even two!"

I got in the car and walked up to the box office at The Park Theater on El Camino. "One ticket, please!" I exclaimed.

The small person in the booth smiled. "Senior?" he said.

"Almost!" I said and went in to enjoy the show.

What a wonderful beginning to my dotage! I bought myself a car that didn't leak and began my search for a home of my own.

Only those women who have rented all their lives can understand what it meant to me to find a place that where no landlord could complain about stains on the rug, or tell me his brother had just moved in town and I had one month to get out. Only those single women who thought they would spend their entire lives hauling clothes to Laundromats can know the glory of tripping out to the garage every day to launder anything they wanted to clean.

My new paradise had a real garden; one I could fill with my own roses and honeysuckle. I didn't ever have to leave my flowers to another renter. It was forever mine to love. And I do.

All that happiness came rushing into my life after The Birthday! All I had to do was gather it to my heart. The tears and setbacks of those endless years called youth had been nothing but stepping-stones to my own purple rainbow with the red pot of gold shimmering just for me.

I assure you, my joyous experience isn't unique. Every woman who qualifies for the purple and red of The Better Age feasts at the same banquet I do in my blue and white California castle. And every one of us remembers those bitter lavender years when we never believed our dreams would blossom with such a heady fragrance the moment we hit the mid-century mark. Life does indeed transform tears into laughter and failure into success, the moment we don our purple finery and top it with a bouncy and brilliant red hat.

It's time somebody told you
How much they want, love and need you;
How much your spirit helped set them free
- Keri Hulme

The St. Patrick / Purim Social

Liberality consists in gifts well timed.
- La Bruyere

My senior year in high school, my mother decided that she was going to teach us the real meaning of Purim. "Esther is an excellent example of a strong woman, Lynn Ruth," she said. "She was the one who really saved our people from Haman."

"May I dress like her for the Purim festival Saturday night?" I asked. "I have a great costume. It's green with gold trim."

"The reason we dress up at Purim is to fool Haman into thinking we aren't Jewish," said my mother. "You have to go as something like a horse or a Persian. Maybe you can think of something Friday night, while we bake hamantashen to give to the poor."

"I forgot to tell you I invited Louise Dougherty over that night," I said. "Can she help us?"

"Fine," said my mother. "We are supposed to spread joy to people who are very sad and make them laugh. Can the two of you do that?"

"Could we make a party for the girls at The Florence Crittendon Home for Unwed Mothers?" I asked. "They are really sad over there."

My mother looked puzzled. "Whatever made you think of those girls?" she asked.

"Mrs. Kudzia told us about them today in social science," I explained. "She said they made bad moral judgments and that's why they were pregnant. She said most of them had to give their babies away as soon as they had them and I think that's awful."

My mother nodded. "It is, Lynn Ruth," she said. "I think both of you would be doing a wonderful thing if you brought those girls some laughter at this time in their lives."

"If I was ever lucky enough to have a baby, I would never give it away," I said.

My mother looked very solemn. "Sometimes fate won't allow us to do what our heart wants us to do, Lynn Ruth," she said.

"Can we color some of the hamentashen green for the St. Patrick's Day Bash at Crosby Park Sunday?" I asked. "Louise invited me to go with their family. She says everybody eats corned beef and cabbage and dances to keep from getting gas."

Friday night, I told Louise that Jewish people gave food and money to the needy and made them laugh on Purim. "I thought the perfect place would be The Florence Crittendon Home because those girls are in such trouble."

"I can help you bake the hamantashen and drive you both over there Saturday afternoon," said my mother. "But you'll have to figure out how to make the girls there laugh. I don't think it's going to be easy."

Louise and I gave each other knowing looks. "We can make ANYONE laugh," said Louise.

"Why are they are being punished for making bad moral judgments?" I asked. "Lying is a bad moral judgment, too but no one has to go live in a home and give their baby away for that!"

"We can talk about that after you've met the girls," said my mother. "Let's get started."

"On Purim, the Jews tried to fool Haman by not looking Jewish so I can dress like a leprechaun and Louise can go as Queen Esther," I said.

"But I'm Irish," said Louise.

"Exactly," I said.

The next day, my mother drove us to the home laden with green punch and hamantashen.

"I hope I don't start to cry when I see all those pregnant girls," I said. "I feel just awful for them. If I ended up pregnant every time I made a bad moral judgment, I would probably have to live at that place for a hundred years."

"I think you don't really understand what kind of moral judgments Mrs. Kudzia meant," said Louise "Now get ready to make the girls laugh because here we are!"

The two of us, Louise in a green satin dress with a crown on her blonde curls and me in a velvet leprechaun suit ran up the walk of the home and rang the bell. All the residents gathered in the hall to greet us and when they saw us, they began to giggle. "Look at that cute little leprechaun!" shouted one. "And that other girl has shamrocks all over her gown and a Star of David around her neck!"

"I am Queen Esther with her favorite elf," said Louise. " We want to do a double whammy today and celebrate Purim and St. Patrick's Day together."

"Oh, I just love a party!" said a very small girl who had been watching us, her huge dark eyes big as saucers.

I looked at her and I gasped. She looked like she was about thirteen. Her tummy was so large I thought she would tip over. She walked over to me and hugged me. "I think you are being very lovely to think of others on your holiday," she said. "Don't you love having fun? The trouble with the world is that there are so many things we have to do that there's no time left for cutting up."

"Right!" said Louise. "What's the use of living if you can't enjoy it?"

"What's your name?" I asked the girl.

"Lynn Elaine," she said and I smiled.

"My name is Lynn, too!" I exclaimed and I took her hand in mine. "Will you help me put out the cookies?"

I watched her very carefully as we dusted off the trays and arranged our green little cakes in a pretty circle. I wanted to see what there was about her that made her make bad moral judgments but she didn't do one single thing that was unusual. In fact, she folded the napkins just like I always did and put a doily on the tray before she arranged the pastry. "My mother taught me to make things nice," she said.

"So did mine!" I said. "Do you like to sing?"

"I just love it"" she said. "My favorite singer is Perry Como."

"Mine, too!" I said. "I love to dance too. Louise says it prevents gas."

"What a nice way to do that!" said Lynn Elaine. "My mother always made me take a tum."

* * * *

"Did you have fun?" my mother asked on our way home.

We nodded, our eyes shining with the happy, giggling memory of celebrating two holidays at once with girls who laughed at all our jokes and loved all the same hit records. "I didn't see one single thing different about those girls. They were as ordinary as we are," I said.

"That is the lesson Purim teaches us all," said my mother. "Everyone goes through bad times and it is a blessing for those of us who are doing well to share those difficulties with them. Who knows? Next year we may be in their shoes."

I nodded sagely. "Just because some stupid stork dumps a baby in your tummy is no reason to feel guilty. Birds have lousy morals anyway."

My mother nodded. "What a good lesson to remember!" she said. "Watch out for strange birds or you might get caught."

"Doing what?" I asked.

"We really MUST have that talk," said my mother.

Whatever is done or said returns at last to me.
- Walt Whitman

Thinking It Over

A faithful friend is the medicine of life
- The Bible

Kay Dartt was my neighbor in a trailer park in Oregon, Ohio back in the sixties. During that period of my life, I was nurturing my career as a free lance writer. Whenever I could escape for a walk, Kay's two daughters, Tammy and Michelle joined me and I grew to love them as my own. One day, her husband Paul called to their oldest daughter, "Tammy, its time help your mother make dinner."

The child recoiled from his touch. "I don't have to listen to YOU!" she hissed. "You aren't my father."

Paul flushed as if he had been struck and before I could say anything, Kay grabbed Tammy by the collar, her anger so visible I thought it would ignite us all. "You go into that kitchen this minute," she said. "You don't know how lucky you are that this man is your father."

It was that remark that sparked the conversations Kay and I began having each time we met. I learned a lot about Kay and her background from those discussions and the one thing that amazed me was how strongly we bonded even though we shared no common interest and lived our lives by totally different rules.

"Tammy's real father is in prison this time for car theft," she said. "We went out a few times after he got out for selling heroin. I was about fifteen years old and I thought I loved him. But as soon as I got pregnant, he walked out on me. My mother threw me out of the house and I used to beg on the street for food or rummage through restaurant dumpsters. The two of us slept in the park. Paul married me the year after Tammy was born because he felt sorry for us."

I had always thought that no matter what happened, your parents came to your rescue. But that little rule was only one of several that didn't seem to apply in Kay's life. I couldn't imagine anyone getting pregnant at fifteen much less to a criminal; and no matter how hungry I was, it was beyond the scope of my imagination to picture myself begging for food or sleeping in a park. "Did you have to go to a charity hospital to deliver the baby?" I asked.

Kay smiled at me as if I were a four year old verifying the good fairy. "No hospital," she said. "I was fifteen without a guardian to speak up for me. I thought a long time about what to do and the answer came to me right before the pains began. I had Tammy on my girl friend's couch. She let me stay overnight but then her mother found out about me and I was out on my own again."

This sounded like the stuff of soap opera to me. Where were the social workers hiding? Where was The Salvation Army for heaven sake?
"How did you survive?" I asked.

"You'd be surprised at the things you do when you have to," said Kay. "I always think about my problems right before I go to bed and by morning, I know exactly what to do. I just figure out where they'll be getting rid of food that day or when the big deliveries come at K-Mart and see to it I'm right there to take my share. Paul collects garbage for a living and we hardly make enough to pay for the rent much less the heat and light. It's my job to figure out how we can make it and I always do. "

I said nothing. I had always believed that there was never an excuse for thievery but then I had never been faced with caring for a family with no resources other than my own ingenuity. How can you send a child out in the cold without a coat? How can you put a hungry baby to bed without a blanket to cover him?"

That July, it was so hot that the thermometer descended to 100 degrees after sundown. I had no air conditioning in my trailer and, exhausted from the heat, I stepped on my cat. He retaliated by biting my ankle. The next day my leg turned a greenish yellow and my fever was 106 degrees. I called my doctor and he informed me that if I didn't get into a hospital immediately my brain would be cooked. I called Kay and she drove me to Parkwood Hospital.

I was there the rest of the week with a case of Cat Scratch Fever, a common and harmless result of a cat bite. Kay visited me that Wednesday to present me with an elaborate bouquet of flowers she funded by going door to door in the park and telling my neighbors I had rabies. Neither she nor the other inhabitants of this park realized that had I indeed been so afflicted, they would have been putting those flowers beside a gravestone instead of at my bedside. She handed me an envelope. "We had twenty five dollars left over," she said.

Twenty-five dollars in the sixties was a sizeable amount of cash and this was a woman who got her food from dumpsters in supermarket alleys. Ours was a run down park and the inhabitants had no cash to spare in the best of times. I suspected that much of the money in that envelope belonged to her. "You keep that," I said. "You certainly earned it. "

Kay was shocked. "I couldn't do that," she said. "That money is yours. It doesn't belong to me."

I returned to my mobile home to continue trying to crack the freelance writing market. It must have been September of that year when I finally got my first acceptance from Toledo's major newspaper, THE BLADE. I was assigned several lead stories and I was elated. This could be a real beginning for me, I thought. Perhaps at last I would have enough money to pay for my groceries and drive my automobile. My editor asked me to do a story about the unwed mothers in our park and sent out Jim O'Reilly, the staff photographer to do a photo shoot. Jim was a happy-go-lucky Irishman whose every beverage was ninety proof. The first time he visited my mobile home, he informed me that I was beautiful; his wife didn't understand him and come give us a bit of a cuddle, honey. I was very nervous about this second appointment. I was determined not to spoil my chances with the editor and just as adamant that no frustrated drunk was going to paw me on assignment. "I just don't know how to handle this one," I told Kay during one of our talks.

"Leave it to me," she said. "What time is he coming over?"

"Four this afternoon," I said.

At four o'clock, Jim rang my bell. I could smell him before I opened the door. He reeled into my front hall, arms out to grab me but before he could lunge, the bell rang again and there was Kay's six year old, Michelle licking a candy cane. "Hi, Auntie Lynn," she said. "I'm here to keep you company."

For the next two hours, that photographer and I toured the park taking pictures of the several girls who had had their babies at thirteen and fourteen. I took notes, Jim took pictures and Michelle was inches from my elbow. We took an excellent round of pictures, Jim's behavior was irreproachable and Michelle finished her candy cane and started a second. When Jim left, Michelle smiled at me. "Mother told me I was to follow you wherever you went until the man with the camera went away. Is it okay if I go home now?"

I took her hand and together we went to her house. "You saved my career!" I told Kay. "What made you think of using Michelle as a decoy?"

Kay blushed. "I thought about the problem all morning," she said. "And the answer just came to me," she said. "It always does."

Kay Dartt, a woman who barely finished the sixth grade, taught me a lesson no professor at graduate school ever revealed. Helping someone you love is always possible if you will only take the time to give it a little thought.

There is always an easy solution
to every human problem.
- H. L. Mencken

Voting

The only way to make sure people you agree with can speak is to support the rights of people you don't agree with
- Eleanor Norton

Voting is the most private and personal act I perform. I would no more insist someone join me in the voting booth than I would invite him to accompany me into the bathroom. My vote is an independent decision I make alone. I agonize over all sides of the question and try to consider all the options and then I make up my mind.

I can still remember the first time I entered a polling place. It was the presidential election of 1956. I made a special trip from Cleveland where I was teaching to Toledo, where I had registered to vote and went to the polling place nearest my parents' home because that was my legal residence.

In those days, the voting site was always a short walk from your front door and it was peopled by friendly ladies who sat knitting sweaters, scarves and mittens for their grandchildren until someone came to cast their ballot. They served cookies and punch and knew all of us by name. We all were neighbors after all. I felt as if I had just stumbled into an old fashioned quilting party when I walked through those doors.

Those who arrived at a busy time like early in the morning or right after five o'clock at night, waited their turn and talked about issues like the weather, the catastrophic sinking of the Andrea Doria and the miracle of the Salk vaccine. "Polio will be a thing of the past!" said the woman on my right and I nodded. "Thank heavens for that!" I said. "Have you heard that crazy singer, Elvis Presley? I can't believe people pay good money to hear that caterwauling."

The topics we did not discuss were the candidates or the issues at stake that day. Those subjects were not mentioned within forty feet from the front door of the polling place. Besides, we were tired of hashing and rehashing them. That's all we had discussed for months in our living rooms, around our dinner tables and on our way to the movies or football games.

The 1956 election was a presidential one and very exciting for a first time voter. Adlai Stevenson, idol of every college student across the nation was running against Dwight D. Eisenhower, hero to every veteran of World

War Two. That contest was only one of the many issues I had to evaluate when I entered that small curtained booth. I accepted the stubby pencil and the long paper ballot the ladies handed me and after they drew the curtains around me, I took time to rehash every decision I had made before I left the house that afternoon. I sincerely believed that casting my vote was the most important thing I could do for my country.

I still remembered the holocaust victims who suffered unrelenting abuse of their personal liberties. I was determined to protect the rights we have in this country by making educated decisions. My judgments may not have mattered one whit to anyone else, but each was momentous for me, one I took seriously, and still do to this day.

I read up on all the issues, listen to every argument and attend informational meetings sponsored by the League of Women Voters. I assure you, I am as well prepared on the First Tuesday in November as I ever was for a final examination in a college course. When I enter that small solitary voting chamber, no matter how torn I am by doubts before I close the curtains around me, I force myself to take a stand. There is no maybe on that ballot; only yes or no.

I rarely discuss my votes with others because for some reason, nothing inflames tempers as fast as someone discovering that you voted for a different candidate or didn't approve his favorite bond issue. I really can't understand their rage. In my opinion, they should feel refreshed by a new outlook. I believe the strength of our country depends on a kaleidoscope of thought, rather than the single rule common to a dictatorships. When I studied government in college, I was taught that the very essence of democracy is the power to cast an individual vote, determined by nothing but your own conscience.

I always believed that everyone took his or her franchise as seriously as I did until I was in Wimberley, Texas and hadn't had a permanent place of residence for over two years. There was another presidential election that year and I was ashamed and heartsick that I couldn't have my say in who became our president. Ronald Reagan was running against Jimmy Carter and I was absolutely certain everyone with a grain of sense would vote for Carter. Ronald Reagan was an actor, for heavens sake. I discussed my inability to make my voice heard to a young man who obviously didn't consider the issues as important as I did. He smiled as he listened to all the reasons I felt Jimmy Carter was the man to save our country and he smiled. "Oh hogwash," he said. "No one really cares about all those ideals of yours. It didn't take me but a minute to decide which man would get my vote."

I was amazed. "Really!" I said. "And which one did you choose?

"I'm voting for Ronald Reagan," he said. "If he can't get the government to do right, at least he can sing and dance."

I was horrified. "You mean that's all you expect from our leaders?" I asked. "Entertainment?"

He nodded. "I don't see what else they've given us."

Many years have passed since that election. Polling places are not so personal anymore. There are voting machines to speed up the procedure and many of us send in absentee ballots to express our opinions. When these ballots are sent to us we receive written statements from each candidate and learned expositions on the pros and cons of each bond issue. Although each party sends us a list of the candidates and issues they endorse, I insist on doing my own homework. Whenever someone gives me a slate of officers and tells me to vote for every name on the list, I automatically suspect it. "I don't know anything about those people," I say. "I don't know what they stand for."

Local issues demand even more homework for me than national decisions. The school boards, the city councils, the water board in my hometown affect me far more immediately than the person in the White House. I read the paper, I talk to my neighbors and I listen to as many discussions as I can about where to put the new library and who should rule the Art Guild. I would not dream of voting for a predetermined group of officers. It is far too simple and it precludes thinking. If voting were that easy, it would be a regular habit in places where the individual has no voice at all.

Thank goodness elections are reserved for humane, democratic countries that fiercely protect each citizens' right to have a separate voice in the laws that govern them. After all, only the guys who cannot put in their two cents have a right to complain about the result. That is what this country is about, isn't it?

Eternal vigilance is the price of liberty
- Wendell Phillips

Who Made the Hummingbirds?

Life is a rainbow
Which also includes the black
- Yevtushenko

A flock of hummingbirds have come to live in my garden for Christmas this year. They hover outside my window, tiny quivering miracles of the creation. I gaze at the prisms of light shimmering on their wings and remember my friend Heléne. I last spoke to her in her hospital room while she ate what might well be her final meal here on earth. I sat beside her while we discussed the human condition and her vision of the hereafter. Her body has been battered from radiation treatments during two victorious struggles with cancer and cannot do its work easily any more. She is eager to leave the discomfort she has endured for so long and has refused to resort to life support systems to prevent her lungs and her digestive system from grinding to a halt. She is certain that she will breathe easier when she can leave her body at last and tread the celestial path to heaven. She has felt God's presence in her life and has no doubt that He will guide her to a better place very soon. The beauty of our world reassures her of His presence. "If there is no God," she said to me. "Who made the hummingbirds?"

There are so many questions in this life that have no answer. Who can explain music that fills us with the hope and peace of mind that no human being can equal? Who can describe the power of love? Why is giving, getting and taking all too often a loss?

Modern life is so crowded with activity that we tend to neglect the reason for our pursuits. The money we make is not our purpose in life. It is only a means to a fulfillment we think we are too busy to seek. We jump out of bed, still groggy with sleep, bolt what breakfast we can prepare so fast that we hardly remember its flavor and drive into the morass of the morning commute. At this time of year, our calendars are packed with events that bring us together with friends we haven't seen in years without a moment to renew our connection with them. We smile, we greet each other with protestations of a love only remembered but no longer felt. The business of life keeps us separated from those we care about and often our contact with them diminishes to a yearly meeting around a holiday punch bowl. This is the season where every spare minute is spent shopping in crowded stores and forcing our way through hordes of people to buy gifts that mean nothing for the family and friends we do not have time to enjoy. We forget that a tie or bottle of perfume is not love. A card is a fleeting thought, not the connection we all need to make life the rich banquet it can and should be for us all.

We all seek this link to a significant other but that kind of deep connection between two souls is not an instant thing. Attraction is, but that alone isn't enough to sustain the sense of loving and being loved that nurtures us and gives life its human dimension. I had occasion to walk with a young lady half my age not long ago and we discussed the need we all share for this bond. "Dating services, e-mails, bar hopping…none of that works for me, " she said. "I've tried to find what I need in every kind of church, but that isn't working either. I need more than friendly people I only see for an hour once a week. I need a spiritual experience that takes me out of myself. That doesn't happen for me at potluck suppers or on committees to beautify the lawn. I want to find a relationship that lasts with someone I care about who can make a difference in my life."

"That's what I call love," I said. "When two people together are more than they are apart. It's that magic that happens when you can feel another's pain; when someone else's joy is what makes you happy. It is a caring that transcends possession. When that happens, we glimpse heaven."

Indeed, at this time of year it is good to think a bit about creating that kind of paradise here on earth. Every time we make another smile, we have burnished him with human gold. Every time we kiss a lonely person and open our arms to give him warmth, we have added feathers to our own wings. Our love has made the moment magic one. It has transformed a lonely room into a thing of beauty.

The spark of life within us is our most precious gift. It only flourishes when we share it with others. And like all prized possessions, we must know when to let it go. Heléne Dunbar has the wisdom and the courage to know when her time to depart is here. She has the faith she needs to know that she is not severing her bond with her husband and two sons. She is only putting it on hold until they join her. She is ready to say her farewell to the earthly existence that no longer gives her pleasure. "I think I have that right," she said. "I told my husband and my son that is the way I want it to be and they have accepted it."

She stood up and we kissed. I waved goodbye to her as if she were on her way to a grand and exciting event and perhaps she is. "Good night, Heléne," I said and the tears welled in my eyes. "I will call you on Thursday."

She nodded. "I 'm not sure where I'll be," she said.

"I'll find you," I said. "If you don't answer the phone, I'll look in that magic garden where they made the hummingbirds and all that is beautiful here on earth, and you'll be there."

Go placidly amid the noise and the haste
And remember what peace there may be in silence
- The Desiderata